Praise for

Farmingdale Gentlemen's Club

A super second book in the *Farmingdale Gentleman's Club* series...full of tense, thrilling action sequences and a delightfully snarky British hero...this was a fabulous rollicking ride from start to finish. ~ *Jessewave Reviews*

The action and suspense kept me rapidly turning pages, my grip weakening with each near miss, each bullet loosed, and each caress given. All combined to ensure that I will be waiting eagerly for the next book in the *Farmingdale Gentleman's Club* series! ~ *Fallen Angel Reviews*

Total-E-Bound Publishing books by T.C. Blue:

Farmingdale Gentleman's Club
A Game of Chances
A Game of Skills
A Game of Hearts

Farmingdale Gentleman's Club

A GAME OF HEARTS

T.C. BLUE

A Game of Hearts
ISBN # 978-0-85715-772-0
©Copyright T.C. Blue 2012
Cover Art by Lyn Taylor ©Copyright January 2012
Interior text design by Claire Siemaszkiewicz
Total-E-Bound Publishing

A GAME OF HEARTS

Dedication

This book is dedicated with many thanks to all those who've asked when it would be out. It's also dedicated to those giving the Farmingdale Gentleman's Club a first try.
Thank you all, so very, very much.

Chapter One

"Okay, seriously? This is so not what I signed up for." He was complaining. River even knew he was complaining. He didn't much care, though. The last thing he'd even considered when he and his sister, Moon, had decided to test with the Farmingdale Gentleman's Club was that he might end up where he was — butt-naked and ass up on a cold table while some nameless guy slathered slickness on his ass. Why was he doing this again?

"You can stop whining any time," the man said, his hands still moving, still getting the job done. "Besides, you'll be thanking me soon. You know what I'm about to do. It'll hurt without the goop."

River grunted and pushed his hips against the table, trying to get away from the careful but still firm touches. "It doesn't exactly feel good, even with it."

A snort. "Lord, you guys are all the same. You act tough, but the minute something gets a little bit uncomfortable, you start bitching and moaning. Now, hold still. This won't take long if you'll just shut up and let me do it. Then you can go cry about how abused you are."

The guy chuckled and River seriously considered stopping him. Except he was right. It didn't hurt as much as it had when they'd started. In fact, it was starting to feel almost good. "Fine," River grumbled, pillowing his head on his arms. "Go ahead. Do it. It's not like I have all day."

"You sure you're ready?" More of the cool, slick substance touched his bottom and River sighed as the careful spreading made it warmer. "I really don't want to hurt you any more than I have to."

"I know, okay? Just…get it done, since you're so damned insistent." He winced at the first sharp pressure, felt the burn. "Don't stop. Just…fuck, man. Go for it."

The guy made a sound then, but River couldn't tell if it was annoyed or amused. "Don't rush me." Okay, amused, River decided. "I'm actually really good at this, or so I've been told. So just lie still and let me take care of you, got it?"

More sharp burning, and River closed his eyes and just breathed through it, slow and steady, body held tense and tight, though he knew it wasn't helping.

"Okay. I'm done." Fuck. Finally. "Let me get you cleaned up and you can be on your way." Soft, damp cloth and a slight citrus scent, soothing his sore ass, and that was actually nice. "Okay. You can get up now."

River grunted and rolled carefully on to his side, then flipped his long blond braid back over his shoulder. "My pants are kind of messed up. Any chance of some scrubs or something?"

The nurse chuckled and tossed thin, folded fabric at him from across the room. "I still can't figure out how you managed to land ass-first in a fireplace, but at least we got the blisters lanced before they went fully septic. The antibiotic ointment should keep them from coming back, but you'll need to apply it three times a day for the next week. Also, you want to let the affected area get as much air as possible. And keep it clean."

River sighed and climbed gingerly from the examination table, making a face when the paper stuck to his skin. "Yeah, yeah. Keep my ass covered in gel and let it all hang out. Got it, man." He pulled on the scrub pants, easing them carefully over his burned rear. "That'll be a big hit up on the Ranch, huh?"

"We'll all try to restrain ourselves," he heard from behind him and River couldn't help grinning when he turned to the door. "Now, come on. You've got debriefing."

River laughed. "I think I'm about as debriefed as a guy can get, man. And this dude just told me I'm supposed to stay naked as much as possible, so briefs? Not so much."

The too-pretty man in the doorway shook his head even as his laugh joined River's. "Bad puns must mean you're feeling better. Come on, River. Report, then you can head on up. I'm sure your usual room is ready and waiting."

"Good," River muttered, relieved. "I'm telling you, Marcus. I could use a little downtime. This last Game." He shook his head at the man he'd come to know fairly well over the last year or so. This mission in the field had been particularly difficult for River this time around.

"Maybe I'll tell you tonight. Unless you and Tanner have plans, dude."

They might, River figured. Marcus and Tanner were both busy guys; they had to find alone-time when they could. The last thing River would ever do was get in the way of that. Well, unless they asked him to, he thought with a grin as he followed Marcus from the room, moving slowly out of deference to his poor, burned ass.

Marcus glanced back and River figured the guy must have seen his wince because Marcus slowed down to walk beside him. "No special plans, Riv. Why don't you come to dinner at the house? Cook's making steak." He smirked. "Or he is since they called up to say you were on-site and injured. We'll even let you eat on the couch so you can lie on your side."

Right, River reminded himself as he and Marcus made their way to the elevators outside Med. That was why he did it. The sense of family. Like he wasn't just another Gentleman, as the FGC called their male operatives, but a friend, too. It pretty much made it all worthwhile.

* * * *

"Oh, come on, Marcus! He fell into a fire!" It was stupid, not to mention sloppy, and Tanner had no idea why his lover couldn't see that. "Last time, he let some woman stab him, and the time before that? He 'accidentally' poisoned himself. *After* the Game Over! He's either incompetent or he has the worst luck in the world!"

Or River was deliberately letting things happen just so he'd be sent to the Ranch to recover. The above-ground facility appeared to be a working ranch, which would afford River the chance to recover from the Game. It would also enable him to spend time with

Marcus, but Tanner couldn't say that. Hell, he couldn't even explain why he felt that way. Probably because River was so damned good looking. River was Marcus' height, strong and tanned, with blue eyes and that long fucking blond hair, all the way down to his butt...and young. River and Moon, aka the Stone Twins, had just turned twenty-four.

River was one of *those* guys, Tanner knew. The kind that other guys looked at. The kind that even straight men wanted on a level they usually wouldn't admit to without threats. Hell, it was almost impossible *not* to at least look at the young man, and Marcus definitely looked. Tanner did too, which didn't make things any better. At all. He trusted Marcus; of course he did. And he didn't have any reason to be jealous, Tanner told himself sternly. Marcus treated River like a kid brother. Marcus was even laughing at what Tanner had just said.

"I'm going with unlucky," Marcus answered as he wrapped his arms around Tanner from behind. "I mean, consider his name alone. River Stone? It's not as bad as Moon Stone, sure, but still." He laughed. "And I haven't seen him in the field, babe, but he's fucking amazing in training and you know it. Almost as good as you are." A soft, light kiss against his neck had Tanner smiling. "But you're more fun to watch," Marcus murmured, the words brushing Tanner's skin as gentle gusts of warm air. "You move like water, Tanner. Liquid. Smooth. You just flow, lover. It's insanely fucking hot."

Well, that was true enough, Tanner figured. At least, Marcus did tend to drag him off as soon as possible after they'd trained together, especially at hand to hand. And Marcus was wrapped around him, touching him, rather than staring out of the dining room window at River where the young man was lying on a blanket in the back field, naked and on his stomach.

Then Marcus' hands slipped lower, pushing into the front of the loose silk pants Tanner had pulled on after showering, and he forgot all about River of the smooth, tanned skin and long blond hair.

"You're pretty damned hot yourself, honey," he murmured, raising one hand up and behind, cupping the back of Marcus' head to hold that soft, wicked mouth to his skin. "Oh. That's good..."

"Just 'good', babe?" Marcus whispered, and Tanner arched just a little, pushing his hardening cock into Marcus' grip while his man's other warm hand weighed his balls, fingers stroking, moving slowly. "I must be slipping."

A small gasp as Marcus closed a loose fist around him and Tanner shook his head. "No, honey. God, no. Not...not slipping. Bed?" Please, God. Just let them go to fucking bed, but Marcus was chuckling against his skin and those hands — those wonderful, talented hands — were moving faster.

"I'm thinking right here, Tanner," Marcus whispered. "Right here, right now. It's been months since we've fucked in here." And Tanner's sac was free, suddenly, because Marcus was pushing the silk down, pulling back just enough to let it puddle on the floor and thank God Marcus had practice in getting out of jeans with one hand because Tanner heard the unmistakable sound of a zipper behind him.

"Stay, lover," Marcus said softly and Tanner stayed, though he wanted to follow the hand that had released his cock, wanted to hold on to that heat. Wanted it to hold on to him, more like, he qualified, but Marcus was back already, and that perfect cock was hard, slick against his skin when Marcus pressed close again. "Mmm...better, babe. Now, let me just..."

Tanner moaned, long and deep, as Marcus held him tightly, his spine against Marcus' chest. And when Marcus rocked, shifted against his back, he couldn't do anything but broaden his stance, giving his honey some room. Then that big, blunt tip was pushing at him and Tanner pushed in return, a small, happy sigh leaving him as his hole spread, opened, accepted the slow invasion with relative ease. "Oh, God. Marcus. So fucking hot in me, honey."

A soft groan. "Mmm...and you're still talking, babe. Let's see what we can do about that." A strong hand on his cock again and Marcus pushed deep as Tanner moaned out something short and sharp when the slow slide met his prostate. And Marcus was still pushing, long and thick and hot, filling Tanner just right, just like he always did.

God, it was one of those times. Sudden, but who needed foreplay when Marcus was right there inside him? Three years and while he was used to it, used to Marcus and the strength of him, the thick heat, it was still new, even while being blessedly familiar. "So good," Tanner groaned, clenching his ass tightly around his lover's hefty shaft. "Yeah...like that, honey."

"Just...like...that," Marcus agreed, his voice more grunt than anything else. And his hand was stroking Tanner's turgid flesh, spreading dribbles and drops of fluid, easing the slowly increasing up and down, and Tanner clenched again, holding Marcus deep. "Fuck, babe. Just...oh, yeah. Fuck..."

Faster, just like that, Marcus jabbing in, pulling back—making love to him, Tanner knew—because it was always making love. Even when they were too hot, too ready for anything like easy, it was still making love. Even when it was straight-up-dirty fucking, though this wasn't that. "Oh, God. Soon, honey. Soon." Gasped, because he couldn't seem to catch his breath all of a sudden, but Tanner was used to that, too. Loved it almost as much as he loved Marcus.

"Now, babe," Marcus growled, his teeth finding Tanner's shoulder and latching on hard enough that Tanner knew there'd be a mark, and that was fine, that was perfect. Then that hand around him, sliding down, rough and just what he needed. "Right fucking now."

Tanner let loose something like a cry, something like a sob. He couldn't help it, didn't even want to. His body shuddered, held there between the window and Marcus, Marcus's hand around his cock, that thick shaft plunging deep, and he was already singing, silently and on the inside. Then on the outside as Marcus surged wildly, swelled inside him, pulsed rough heat into him over and over while Tanner spilled white and slick and wet against the glass and Marcus' fingers.

They were silent for a moment, communicating solely with shuddering breaths and pounding hearts, until Marcus slowly pulled back, dragging himself from Tanner's body with obvious reluctance. "You okay, babe?" he whispered and Tanner couldn't help smiling at the so-familiar question.

"I'm great, honey," he answered, turning to wrap Marcus in his arms, the silk still pooled around his ankles making him move carefully. He pressed a long, deep kiss to his lover's mouth, even as he felt Marcus' hands on his back, one sticky, one not. "I think I need another shower, though," he added when the kiss gently ended.

Marcus laughed, dropping one hand to squeeze Tanner's ass. "We both do, babe. And we should probably clean off the window, too. Before the cum dries and turns into glue."

Jesus. Oh, God. He'd completely forgotten about…"Shit, honey. River."

Marcus chuckled even more. "What about him? And should I be worried that mentioning cum makes you think of him?" One dark brow arched at him but Tanner knew Marcus was teasing. It didn't help, though, or at least not much.

"Funny. But I meant…what if he saw us? Oh, fuck. Marcus, he was right outside and…"

A soft snort. "Right outside at least fifty feet away, Tanner. I doubt he was even looking. And if he was?" Marcus grinned then stepped back to pull up denim and tuck himself inside. "Who cares, babe? I'm not ashamed of the way I love you. Besides, you're fucking beautiful when you come." He frowned and crouched, then rose again to drag silk over Tanner's hips. "Well, you're always gorgeous, but especially when you come. For me or in me. Either way, you're fucking stunning."

Marcus nodded and Tanner found himself being turned again to look through the window. "Besides," Marcus added, "he's not even facing the house, Tanner. He didn't see a thing."

Okay. Okay, good. And Marcus was right, Tanner saw. River was on his side, either sleeping or watching the colts in the pasture. It actually helped. "I guess I'll take care of the window, then," he said with a grin. "Meet you in the shower?"

"You'd better, babe." Marcus nodded. "I think you might need me to wash your back. Or maybe you'll wash mine."

Chapter Two

Well, that had been...interesting wasn't the right word, River decided, though it for damned sure hadn't been boring. Shit, looking right through that window, watching Tanner get fucked had been...yeah. Not boring. And knowing it was Marcus making that long body rock until cum splattered the glass was the stuff of fucking wet dreams.

Not that he usually had wet dreams, River reminded himself, staring sightlessly at the grass beyond the fence, one hand resting lightly on his straining cock. He was enough in touch with his own libido that he tended to jerk off at least once before bed, always while imagining whoever might be the current object of his admittedly fickle affections.

It was strange for him to go long without managing to crawl into bed with whoever he was lusting after, granted, but that wasn't really possible, considering. And no matter how hard and ready seeing Tanner like that had him, it wasn't Tanner or even Marcus that River wanted. He thought it might be easier if it were.

Even so, there was no point in wasting a perfectly good erection, River decided, wrapping his fingers loosely around his ready shaft. Some relief, even solitary relief, would be good.

His eyes lifted from the pasture, looking at the clouds passing overhead, and River stroked himself slowly at first, letting the sensations wash over him while imagining dark hair and two pairs of eyes, one set a blue lighter and greyer than his own, the other set brown.

They would look at him like he was something special, River thought, losing himself just a little to the daydream. Like he was fine enough, strong enough to be with them. They would touch him and want him enough that what River did in the field didn't matter. And maybe, just maybe…they'd want him more than once.

"That would be nice," River whispered to the sky, his hand moving faster, more firmly. "Twice, three times…yeah. That would be fucking awesome." He imagined lips on his skin, hands sliding over sweaty flesh, sensations that would drive him crazy. And when he came, River dreamed, it wouldn't be alone.

Except he was, right then. Balls drawn up, tight and hard, cock swelling just a bit more. Entirely alone under sun and sky, but for the horses in the field. That didn't stop him from spilling over his fingers, of course, but River was pretty sure it would feel better with someone else there. Hell, it always did.

"Oh, man," he sighed as he wiped cum-slicked fingers in the grass beside his blanket. "I so need to get laid." Except it wasn't lack of sex that was bothering him, though he hated to admit it even to himself. He had plenty of sex, it was just usually part of the Games, or missions, which he'd known before he'd signed on, so he couldn't really bitch about it after the fact. He just hadn't expected to want anyone more than once. He never had before.

Oh, he wasn't looking for whatever it was that Marcus and Tanner had. River figured he was way too young to even think about that. And he wasn't exactly sure that he would ever want something so...intense and permanent. He *liked* being a big old slut; liked playing around. Women, men, whichever. It was fun. Hot. Felt good. Except when he was caught up in wanting what he couldn't have. Except when even knowing it was hopeless didn't stop the want.

He might not be designed for long-term, serious stuff, but that didn't mean he was the kind of guy who would intrude on someone else's relationship. Especially when there wasn't even a hint of interest from either of the men involved. It sucked, but there it was, damn it.

River settled on the blanket again, face down, and tried to push it from his mind. No point in tormenting himself needlessly, and River was generally happier when he wasn't thinking, anyway. Thinking was overrated, and unnecessary when he wasn't in the field. He would just lie there, he decided, and let the fresh air and sunshine heal his wounded ass.

It was as good a plan as any.

* * * *

"Marcus. How's it going?"

The words were unexpected, as was the voice that spoke them. Enough so to have Marcus looking up from his desk and offering Morgan a surprised smile. "Hey. It's going, I guess." He made a face that hopefully showed irritated amusement. "If you're looking for Patrice, she's checking my work on that storage room she made me clean out." And hadn't that been entirely not fun.

Morgan laughed and shook his head as he came farther into the outer office. "You said something about her and Marshall again, didn't you?" the man said, though it wasn't really a question when Marcus was sure Morgan already knew the answer. "I thought you knew better than that by now."

A small pause, and Marcus was sure Morgan was blushing when he continued. Hard to tell with the deep tan Morgan had. "So speaking of knowing better, how's River doing? Healing up okay from that little, um...stumble he took?" Yeah, definitely a blush. Interesting.

Marcus shrugged. "I doubt he'll be sticking his ass in another fire any time soon, but he's fine." He grinned and closed the folder he'd been organising for Patrice. As Assistant Director and Events Coordinator for the FGC, she commanded their team and others with a ruthless determination that he admired and it wouldn't do to keep her waiting. "Tanner might blister his butt in a whole other way, though. He's getting really tired of River running around the Ranch naked, flapping in the breeze and all." True enough. Tanner was of the opinion that six days was long enough for the constant nudity. Marcus knew because Tanner had said so at least a dozen times just that day.

Morgan laughed at that, though Marcus thought there was a certain tightness around Morgan's eyes that was...odd. "Seriously? Huh. First time I've ever heard of someone wanting the kid to put clothes *on*. Usually the opposite, you know?"

Well, well. Morgan actually sounded just as strange as that odd tightness looked. Sounded sort of insulted and envious, both at once. Again, interesting. Very. Marcus shrugged again and chose his words carefully, just to test his sudden hypothesis.

"Oh, believe me, I know. *I* don't have any problem with River running around in the sun with his butt all slicked up. It's...inspiring." Marcus offered a teasing grin then grinned even more at Morgan's sudden glare. "So tell me. Does Simon know?" Oh, he was going to hell for teasing Morgan, but damned if he could help it. Too easy. Too much fun.

Morgan's brow furrowed, his glare becoming confused in less than a second. "Know what? That River burned his ass? Of course he does. He was running the Game."

Marcus snorted and shook his head. "I meant, does Simon know you have a thing for Riv. Or are you and Simon sharing? Because that would be...well, you know. Hot." Another big grin and Morgan looked appalled.

"I do *not* have 'a thing' for River!" Except Morgan seemed more embarrassed than offended, all of a sudden. "He's just another member of the team, for fuck's sake! Jesus, Marcus!"

"Come on, Morgan," Marcus crooned suggestively as he got up from behind his desk and moved around it, finally leaning against the edge just a foot or so from Morgan's gaping form. "You can tell me. Long nights at the comm, listening to River do what he does...you can't tell me that you resist that pretty body every single time. Or was I right? Do you and Simon *share* the guy?" Marcus grinned as Morgan's mouth opened and closed a few times, no sound emerging. "And is there video, because yeah. I'm pretty sure I could make a killing selling it on the Internet. You and Simon, all tangled up in River's hair while the three of you did dirty, wicked things to and with each other, all sorts of filthy words and sounds filling the air? Especially Simon, with that fun English accent of his. Hmmm…"

Jesus, the idea actually was hot, Marcus realised as the pictures and sounds formed in his mind. He'd have to talk Tanner through it later, just for fun.

"We're not sleeping with River," Morgan growled. "It would be unprofessional, especially in the field, and you know it. And he's only twenty-four, for fuck's sake."

And again with the interesting, Marcus thought, feeling smug. Because whatever Morgan might have meant to say, Marcus noticed that there were no words even approximating the message that the man didn't *want* River. Just that River was young and that mixing business with pleasure was a bad idea.

He had a new mission, Marcus decided, even if it was just to torment Morgan. And Simon, which was always fun. The Brit handled teasing better than Morgan did, anyway. So. Okay.

Marcus let the huge, taunting smile fade to something simpler and more friendly, then he clapped Morgan on one solid, tense shoulder. "I'm just fucking with you, Morgan. Hell, from what I can tell, River doesn't even like guys that much. Which is a damned shame, by the way, because he's fucking pretty."

He winked and Morgan relaxed. Or relaxed as much as he ever did, which wasn't really much. Then again, Marcus figured, the guy had spent seven years before joining the Farmingdale Gentleman's Club running for his life and for the life of Jericho, better known as Rico, who was Morgan's…sort-of daughter. It would likely take a while longer before Morgan would be *able* to really relax, even within the confines of a grey-ops organisation like the FGC. Gentleman or not, Morgan didn't have an easy time of it, even in the Club. Hell, Morgan lived with Simon, and God knew that had to be nerve racking enough. And the sparring sessions, both verbal and physical, between Simon and Patrice...Marcus laughed. "It's cool."

Morgan shook his head slowly, despairingly, it looked like. "You don't have that gaydar shit Simon's always talking about, do you?" Okay, unexpected. "You know how River got his ass burned?"

Morgan leaned closer when Marcus shook his head. "He was with Jenny Canas. You know, Alberto Fiori's daughter. She married Hector Canas and he became her father's second in command?"

"Everyone knows that, Morgan," Marcus answered easily. "And River and you both went to that party Fiori threw because we needed to get our skewed intel on the Giordano family to his ears without anyone suspecting." He almost added a *duh*, but that would have been childish.

"Well, River decided the best way to do that was to go through the daughter." Morgan chuckled softly. "So he seduced her. They were in the middle of things when Hector, Jenny's husband, walked in on them."

Okay... "And all River got was a burned ass? I'm impressed."

Morgan snorted. "Seems the Canases have a few secrets they're not so gung-ho about Jenny's dad knowing. Like...when Hector walked in on them, Jenny was giving it to River but good. Had him ass up over the arm of a couch, still in his tux jacket and shirt. So she was fucking him with a strap-on moulded from a very famous porn star's cock and Hector wanted in on the action, so he dropped trou and jammed his dick down River's throat."

What the fuck? "No way," Marcus breathed, but Morgan sounded so matter of fact, Marcus couldn't really doubt it. "Wait. How does that put River in the fireplace? It was a fireplace, right?"

A laugh, low but real. "After the first round, Hector decided he wanted some of what his wife had, so there they were, River bent forward and holding on to the mantel, Hector giving it to him good and hard, and Jenny watching from the couch. Next thing River knows, Jenny's saying someone's coming and Hector's across the room getting himself dressed again. Only problem is, he caught River's foot when he was moving and River somehow got spun around, lost his balance and…"

God, Marcus was laughing too, all of a sudden. He could just picture it. "Oh, fuck. Just…fuck. Poor River."

"Yeah," Morgan agreed. "You really should have seen it, man. River rolling around, no pants, rubbing his ass on the carpet like a dog in heat; Hector standing there half-dressed with a condom hanging off his prick. And meanwhile, Jenny was just sitting there looking cool and calm, like she didn't have a fucking harness and rubber cock under her ball gown. It was fucking priceless."

Shit, it sounded like it. "And River told you all that?" Fuck, Marcus would have lied his ass off if it had happened to him.

"Not exactly," Morgan said, still chuckling. "See, Jenny really did hear someone coming. It just happened to be me."

"The important part" — Morgan added a few minutes later, when Marcus had mostly stopped laughing — "is that River got the job done and Jenny passed the information along to her father."

"Okay," Marcus agreed. "Okay. But just how hard were you, seeing all that and knowing how it happened?" He grinned even more when Morgan growled.

"About as hard as I'm gonna fucking hit you if you don't stop yanking my chain, man." Even so, Morgan looked amused. "Look, Rico wanted me to stop by and invite you to lunch, but I'm not sure if that's a good idea. I don't want you bringing up that lame shit about me and River around her."

Just like that, Marcus was pushing Morgan towards the door. "She might be the least childlike child I've ever met," Marcus answered, "but I wouldn't do that. Hell, Patrice would kill me, assuming you and Simon left any life in my broken, bleeding body." He winked, though he wasn't entirely kidding. He could probably take Morgan. Maybe even Simon. But the both of them together? They'd wipe the fucking floor with him.

Besides which, Marcus had a sneaking suspicion that Jericho already knew exactly what was going on. The girl was kind of scary that way, and she was only twelve. God help them all when she got older. "Come on," he added, "I'm wanting a hot dog, all of a sudden. In a bun." He ducked Morgan's swat easily, then started down the hall.

Chapter Three

"Right, then," Simon snapped out as yet another long sigh left Morgan's lips. "Princess is sleeping, we're in bed—naked, I might add—and you're acting like it's a chore to be here, love. Bloke could develop a complex if you keep on, yeah?" Bloody fucking hell. "So what's crawled up your bum, then? Might as well have it out so's I can put it to rights."

Another sigh and Morgan was on his side, meeting Simon's gaze with those deep brown eyes that always seemed to peer into Simon's soul. "It's nothing," Morgan said, sounding grumpy, the daft git. "Just some stupid shit Marcus was saying. I'm fine."

Simon snorted and reached out, grabbing Morgan's arm and pulling him down against his own leaner form. "Must be they've changed the meaning of 'fine' since the last time I checked. Come on, love. Tell Simon what's running about in that twisty brain of yours, yeah?" He shifted just a bit, hoping to arrange Morgan more comfortably for both of them, then let one hand trail slowly up and down Morgan's ribs. "If it helps, love, bloody Marcus works for 'bitchy-bitch' Patrice. Might be her brand of affection's worn off on him. So what did the tosser have to say, then?"

"Like I said, it's stupid bullshit," Morgan answered with a soft sigh, though it wasn't like the others. In fact, the new sigh sounded contented, like Morgan was happy to be right where he was, which Simon didn't mind at all. "We were talking about River and...Marcus has some weird idea that we're fucking him. River. Uh, you and me, I mean."

"Well, that's just bollocks," Simon said simply, still stroking Morgan's skin. "Not saying I'd mind, granted. Stone's a good looking bloke. Seems a good bit more drawn to you than me, though."

Morgan was suddenly tense against him, Simon realised. In fact, Morgan was looking at him like he'd gone and sprouted horns when Simon turned his eyes from the ceiling and met wide, baffled brown with his own greyish blue. "What, love?"

"I...I thought...I mean, we don't. Or do we and I just didn't know?" Well, Simon figured that had made some sort of sense to Morgan, though Simon was more than a bit in the dark. "I. You. Have you? I mean, before? And I was just...stupid and didn't see it?" Morgan added, and still not a single sodding clue on Simon's part.

He must have looked as confused as he was because Morgan frowned and the next thing Simon knew, his bloke was on him, straddling his waist while Morgan held Simon's wrists up on the mattress to either side of his head. "Have you been fucking around, Simon?" Morgan growled the question and it was so unexpected, Simon laughed.

He laughed loud, the sounds pushing from him as though forced by something inside. Possibly his heart, because it was pounding so fiercely all of a sudden. And Morgan was staring at him, brown eyes deeper, hotter than usual, though there was anger there and something else that Simon didn't like. Something that looked an awful lot like sorrow or maybe just hurt. Bloody hell, he'd gone and hurt Morgan's feelings without ever planning it or trying. Sod it all.

"'Course not, love," Simon said, laughter fading away and leaving only surprise behind. "I've not even given it a real thought, to be honest. Right caught up in you, nobody else." Morgan's stare got harder, like he was trying to decide whether to believe Simon's words and that was...bloody well insulting. "Would have said so, pillock. If I was thinking about it, yeah? And I'm right offended that you'd even think that, wanker. Might not make with the talking about shit so much, but I'd for bloody damned sure have mentioned *that*."

Morgan still didn't look sure, but at least some of the suspicion appeared to have faded, and that was good. "You said...you said you wouldn't mind fucking River, Si. Said he was..." Morgan swallowed and Simon got it. Pinned to the bed, wrists held tightly in Morgan's hands, he got it.

A simple smile spread over Simon's lips and he nodded as he rocked beneath Morgan's straddling form. "Said he's an attractive enough bloke, yeah. Also said I've seen the way he watches you when you're not looking, love. Doesn't mean I'm spreading myself about, does it?" Simon rocked again, letting Morgan feel his cock firming under Morgan's heated flesh. "Can't say as I'd mind watching, or even being part of it, should something come of the attraction you're so bothered by, but that's something we can talk to death later. For the record though? I know where we stand. And nobody can bloody well change that. Not even the Stone boy."

"Okay," Morgan answered, his body shifting back and forth just a bit, though Simon wasn't sure Morgan was aware of it. "Okay. I'm just...I guess I'm still not used to this, Si. I don't..."

Simon snorted and pushed against Morgan's hands lightly. "If the next words out of your daft gob have anything to do with not deserving blah-blah-blah, I'll have to remind you which of us is the sodding senior Gentleman. Now, love. You've got me pinned, here. What are you planning to do with me?" He arched his brows and let his smile turn wicked, taunting just a bit. "Still slick, you know. From before we started this little chat. Might be you could slip right in without even letting go of my hands."

Bloody hell, that was a good look on his man. Like Morgan hadn't even noticed getting hard while they'd been...whatever the fuck it was. Talking, Simon supposed. Naked talking with Morgan on top of him, which was possibly the best kind.

"I could," Morgan said, sounding a bit stunned as he looked down, presumably at his own dick. "Fuck." Well, yeah. That was the idea. Seemed a pity not to. Morgan's erection could be put to good use. It would definitely be blissful, and Simon knew it. It always was.

"Well, then. Get on with it, love." Simon smirked. "Have a shot at wearing me out, why don't you?"

Warm lips met his as Morgan leant down and drove that wet, mobile tongue into Simon's mouth. Moans fed back and forth while Morgan caught up with his body. Then strong thighs moved, pushing between Simon's legs, and Simon spread wide, his knees drawing up to grip Morgan's ribs as Morgan shifted, shimmied a little, then lined himself up and pressed forward, pushed deep. And all the while, that kiss went on, filling Simon's senses and adding to the sweet surrender of his body to his love's.

Minutes passed, harsh breaths gusting from nostrils, mouths devouring slowly, deeply, bodies rocking together and apart in waves of slow desire, and as unexpected as the tenderness was, considering what had led to the moment, it was welcome. Wanted. Needed and desired. Simon swallowed Morgan's moans, locked his ankles at the small of Morgan's back, and gave himself over to sweat and heat and musk...and when Morgan's skin brushed his leaking cock one more time, Simon fed a soft groan into their kiss and scented the air with his own fulfilment, Morgan following close behind.

"*That's* where we stand, love," Simon murmured against Morgan's hair a good while later, his hands finally freed to roam slowly over Morgan's back. "And not a single thing will ever make it anything but so. Could fuck a million other blokes, the both of us, and it wouldn't do a single thing to change what we are, Morgan. Not a bit."

Morgan smiled slightly. Simon felt it against his neck. "You'd really want to watch?" he asked, sounding so careful, Simon almost wanted to smack him. "If you were right about River. And me. You'd want to see?"

Simon chuckled. Quietly, so as not to disturb the sense of peace and ease they'd somehow created between them so unexpectedly. "Would I want to be there while my bloke split someone wide with his perfect sodding cock? 'Course I would, love. Sit nearby, have a bit of a wank...wait for one of you to invite me in." He grinned and pressed a kiss to

Morgan's head, then pushed a hair from his mouth with his tongue. "Not saying it has to happen. Ever. But if it's something you decide you'd like to have a go at? Wouldn't complain, love. Up to you."

Morgan grunted just a bit and shifted, and Simon let out one low sigh as the motion had that big, softened cock slipping fully from him. "I...can I think about it, Si?" Morgan asked with a yawn. "I don't know how I feel about that. Not yet."

"Think all you like, love. Sleep first. Long day tomorrow. Love you, you know."

"Mmm...you too, honey. You too."

Morgan slipped into slumber first, right there on Simon, and that was good. In fact, Simon thought as he closed his eyes, it was bloody well perfect.

They'd talk later. Whenever. After Morgan had had time to think. After Simon had had time to get Marcus into the sparring ring. He wasn't sure yet of how badly he was going to beat the prat, but Marcus deserved at least a bit of discomfort for making Simon's bloke so sodding uncomfortable. Even if it had possibly worked to their advantage.

* * * *

"Well, well. Aren't you looking all healed up."

River jumped, as much as he could while lying naked on a blanket, then squeezed his eyes shut. Fuck. Simon. At the Ranch. Looking at him. Shit. Hello, boner.

"Doc said two weeks," River answered, shifting just a bit to make room for his hardening cock between his body and the blanket. "I'm supposed to have four more days."

Simon snorted and River could picture it, right there behind his closed eyelids. Of course he could. Simon tended to snort a lot; especially around River and even Moon. "You do, mate. Just find it interesting that Doc Pritchard didn't say anywhere in your file that you were required to stay bloody well naked the whole time, bits and bobs flying about. In fact"—Simon added, sounding smug and amused and too damned hot for River's comfort—"you could have gone back to clothing after four days. Blisters weren't that bad, and we both know it."

"Oh, bite me," River grumbled, fully erect against the soft blanket over the grass. "Why were you looking at my med file, anyway? And what are you doing up here, man? Don't you usually keep yourself down in the dungeons?" And please let it be something Simon could explain quickly. Explain quickly, then leave. Jesus, River was screwed up when just the guy's voice had him hard and ready. More than screwed up, because there was no chance.

"I was looking at your file, mate, because I can." Damn, Simon's voice was getting closer. And…shit, River actually felt the small impact when Simon sat down next to him on the fabric. Shit. "Thought I should check up on you, what with me being your bloody handler and all."

That wasn't helping. Not even a little. Not when River could think of all sorts of ways he'd like Simon to handle him; Morgan too. Ways that had nothing to do with Games or the Club. "I'm fine," River managed to say, but fuck if his voice wasn't strained. Strained and tight, just like his body was from resisting the urge to rock against the ground, to search for friction and release, which he couldn't do with Simon right there, damn it. Anyone else, sure. But Simon or

Morgan? Not a chance. "I'm fine," he repeated, "so you can go. I'll be below again soon." Down in the bowels of HQ, where most of the FGC was located. River called it the dungeon.

A chuckle, low and wicked and somehow hotter than sin, and River could imagine Simon shaking his head. "I'll go when I'm good and ready, pet. Seems like you might have done more damage than Doc thought, seeing as you're still parading about in the buff, as it were. Best if I get a closer look."

Oh, for... Shit, that was Simon's hand. On his ass. Fuck. "I. Okay. Okay!" River yelped. "Maybe I just don't want tan lines! My ass is fine!"

Another chuckle, and Simon's hand was moving, rubbing his skin and River tensed even more. He couldn't help it. "Right you are, mate. It's a fine ass you've got." River shivered, which was apparently some sort of signal because he heard Simon moving, then the man's words were right there in River's ear, low, quiet, and somehow more intense for that.

"I think you like flaunting yourself, River," Simon murmured, that hand still moving, sliding up and down and squeezing just a little bit. Just enough to have River panting. "Think you enjoy it, in fact. Gives you a great sodding rush, doesn't it?" And there were fingers sliding lightly down his crack, teasing the sensitive skin there. Fingers slick with the tanning oil River had spread so carefully over his own body. Slender, teasing fingers that River couldn't ignore any more than he could ignore Simon.

He opened his eyes and tried not to groan when Simon leaned closer, catching his eyes. Yeah, River thought, grey-blue. Lighter than his own. So fucking pretty, up close. "What the hell are you doing, Simon?" he demanded, his own voice thick and rougher than River had expected. Then one of those wickedly sliding fingers pushed between his cheeks, twisted to find his hole and River gasped, hips moving deliberately, pushing back and begging for more.

Oh, fuck, Simon could smirk. Simon could smirk and make it look fucking sexy. "Now, now, pet. Run enough of your Games that you *know* what I'm doing, yeah? Seen you looking at my bloke, as well, though Morgan seems to think you've looked on me with a fair bit of want, too." Another wicked little laugh as Simon's finger moved away then returned, teasing River's body shamelessly. "Wasn't sure he wasn't imagining it, though I do admit I'm a bloody stunning bloke in my own right. So. Tell me, River."

"T-tell you what?" River groaned, body still moving, pressing back, pushing forward to rub his cock against the swiftly dampening blanket beneath him. "Fuck, man. Fuck!"

"What, right here? Bit of a great sodding exhibitionist, are you?" Oh, he was so going to punch Simon right in that fucking smug-as-shit mouth. Soon, River promised himself. "I'm not saying no, but I need you to tell me. Is it me you're wanting, or my bloke?" Then that teasing finger pressed again and River gasped, arching hard when just the tip stretched his hole. "Might be both, from the way you're acting," Simon said, sounding like they were having a fucking conversation or some shit. Fuck.

River groaned, legs spreading just a little, and when Simon laughed, River groaned again. "Damn it, man, stop fucking teasing." It was a demand, but it sounded more like a whined plea, even to River. Fuck.

Simon laughed again and shook his head, but that finger did push a little bit deeper. It was more a taunting than relief, damn it. "Is that it, pet? I think it is. You want to be between us, River. Morgan filling your tight little hole with that sodding bludgeon he calls his cock...me slipping between your lips, sliding down your throat. Be a right pretty picture, that. Plug you up, mate, nice and full, no way to speak except with whatever showed in your eyes."

Oh, fuck. Fuck. Simon's finger, deeper still, thrusting in, then pulling back, pushing farther every time. It felt dirty, out there in the open with Simon fully dressed beside him, his own legs spreading wider, cock throbbing, leaking more than the blanket could absorb. Yeah, River felt dirty in the best way ever. Wanted to be even dirtier. "Please," he gasped and Simon pressed closer, fabric all along River's naked side. Oh, yeah. Filthy-dirty was good.

"How hard are you right now, pet?" Simon purred the words, like he was part cat or some shit and River could only moan. Moan and hump between hand and ground, hoping desperately that he wasn't dreaming...and that Morgan wouldn't be showing up soon to kick his ass.

"I'm betting you're close enough to get your end away within moments." Fuck, Simon's voice was hot. Amused. Smooth. "'Course, imagining my bloke deep inside's been known to do it for me, a time or two. Fucks like a bloody machine, Morgan does. He'd open you so wide, mate. Feel him for days, you would. All that bloody heat and strength, just ploughing into your ass, driving your mouth right on to my prick. Think you'd like that just as much as you'd like to fuck me."

Oh, for fuck's sake. Fuckity-fuck. That was it. All she wrote. Because River couldn't help it. Couldn't help the way his body clenched, shoved back wildly to take

Simon's finger as deep as possible. Couldn't help jerking against the wet fabric beneath his cock, or hold back the strangled cry that left his lips as he exploded roughly, eyes and mouth wide.

"I do like a responsive bloke," Simon said then, still looking and sounding smug as he sat up. "Might have to try that again sometime. With less clothes and more walls, of course. I'm not much of one for putting on a show when it can be avoided."

Huh. River blinked, heart still racing, then he felt himself starting to laugh. It felt good, though, so he just let it loose as he shook his head and rolled to sit cross-legged on the blanket in front of Simon, leaving the wet spot to hopefully dry in the sun. "It's not that I don't appreciate the orgasm, man," he said when he'd finished laughing, "but what the fuck brought that on? I was pretty sure you guys had one of those weird exclusive things happening."

Simon shrugged and gave him a grin that River felt from head to toe. Suggestive. Leering. Oh, hell yeah. "We do. Been that way from the start, if you must know. Doesn't mean we can't make room for a bit of play every now and again, yeah?"

Simon arched a brow, just one, and River mirrored the gesture. "Yeah." Easy to say it when he felt it so deep. "Two things, man," River said, arms stretching back, hands on the grass beyond the edge of the blanket holding him up. "It's just playing. Nothing hot and heavy. Nothing that'll mess with the job."

A snort, then Simon was rolling his eyes. "Just a bit of fun, mate. Sweat and skin and buggering till we're sore." Okay, River could do that. Easily. "Understand this, though," Simon went on. "Doesn't matter what we get up to in the sack. In the field, I'm still your superior, got it? That doesn't bloody well change."

That was actually a relief. Simon was his handler, after all. River counted on him to call Game Over, if necessary, based on all the intel, rather than just what River might know during his Play. "Cool, man. So, the other thing. I'm really into being safe. Not just in Games, okay? I mean, you and Morgan. You go without, right? I'm not gonna do that, dude. I trust you guys, but that's not my thing. Cool?"

Oh, man. That was a fucking amazing smile. Like...real and shit. "Cooler than you could ever imagine," Simon answered. "What me and my bloke do is just that, yeah? Us. Know you've not got anything to pass along, so we'll maybe negotiate the whole rubbers for sucking at a future date. Condoms taste fucking awful. But safe is brilliant, pet."

"Good."

Simon's gaze slipped past him then. "Well, guess our little chat is over. Bloody security's headed this way."

River turned and sat up fully, then waved to the big, scarred man approaching from around the side of the main house. "He bothering you, Riv?"

River grinned and shook his head. "Nah, Zeke. It's cool. Simon's my handler. We were just talking about playing." In more ways than one, but Zeke didn't have to know that.

Zeke stood there for a few seconds, then nodded slowly. "Okay. Anyone bothers you, I'll take care of it."

"I know, Zeke. Thanks, man, but I'm fine."

Simon was blinking as the man wandered off. "Well. So that's the infamous Zeke. Sorry to say it, seeing as you're friendly and all, but the bloke seems a bit slow. Still, suppose he gets the job done. Right, then. We'll be seeing you soon, pet." He frowned. "You have rooms down below, I know. What say you get in touch when you've an itch?"

River laughed again. "I'm on sixteen. Blue twenty-seven, man. I might even be down there sooner than four days." He still needed to make sure Morgan was really as on board as Simon said, but he could do that, River decided. Soon. Before he got too attached to the idea that he could actually live out his fantasies at least once. "Later."

He watched Simon go, doubtless headed for the elevator in Marcus and Tanner's house, then laid back on his blanket, letting the sun pour over his tanned front. He grimaced just a bit and shifted away from the dampness he'd left earlier, then released a happy sigh as he closed his eyes again, one hand covering his crotch while the other pillowed the back of his head. "Things are looking up," he announced to the sky, or maybe whatever horses were close enough to hear.

Hell, yeah. Things were definitely looking up.

Chapter Four

"Damn it, Morgan, pay attention!" The voice rang stridently, or maybe it was just his head. "You haven't gone down that easy since you got here. Now get your ass up, shake it off, and focus!"

Well, Tink had a point, Morgan admitted. He'd made a damned stupid rookie mistake and she'd put him down with a simple sidekick, of all things. Fucking stupid. "Sorry, Lady," he grunted as he rolled to his feet, ears still ringing from the fall. The fall he'd taken wrong, damn it, which was yet another amateurish mistake Morgan couldn't afford even once. "I'm feeling kinda off today."

Christ, the woman was scary when she glared like that, which never ceased to amaze him. At five foot nothing and maybe a hundred pounds, tops, Tink was tiny. Tiny and blonde and should have looked sweet as anything. Yet she could take down anyone in the Club, which actually made sense. Tink was in charge of unarmed combat training for all the Gentlemen and Ladies in the FGC. She'd taken every one of them down more than once, though usually not as easily as Morgan had just allowed.

And he *had* allowed it. He was fucking distracted. Just the way Simon had described finding River up top, all stretched out and... Okay, ow. Morgan stared up from his new spot on the floor and rubbed his chest while Tink's glare got harder. Colder.

"Pay fucking attention, damn it, or the next time you're in the field, you'll end up dead! That's twice in a minute, Morgan. Are you *trying* to piss me off? Because if you really want a couple days down in Med, there are probably easier, less painful ways to go about it! Now get the fuck up and act like you're a Gentleman, damn it!"

"Shit," Morgan grunted. "Okay. Sorry. I'm just..."

Tink shook her head, then tilted her neck from side to side, the cracking sound audible even from three feet away, and that was never a good sign. The woman was getting ready to take things to the next level. "I don't care," she said bluntly as Morgan pushed to his feet. "Whatever it is that has you reacting like a civilian, I don't give a rat's ass any more than someone you might run into in the field would. The only difference is that I'm less likely to kill you. So put it away, Morgan. Unless you really do want a Med Sec vacation while your bones heal."

Okay. Okay, she really would break things. Morgan knew that. It wasn't common, but if Tink really thought that was what it would take to get his head in the game, she'd break bones, just to give him something to think about while he recovered. He couldn't really blame her, either. Though Morgan's team didn't usually run into opposition from other agencies similar to the Farmingdale Gentleman's Club, it had been known to happen. And every time a

Gentleman or Lady died, Tink took it personally, like she hadn't trained them well enough or hard enough. Like she could have done more.

It was part of what made her so good at her job, but it still seemed like a hell of a burden for a woman who couldn't be more than thirty or so to bear.

As a secret grey-ops organisation the FGC handled a variety of dangerous, covert operations, and Tink was tasked with training the operatives to a high enough level that they wouldn't get themselves killed. Being off his game could do exactly that and Morgan knew that Tink wouldn't allow it. Morgan shook himself, arms and legs, then cracked his own neck and stepped to the centre of the mat. "You got it, Lady," He answered with a short nod. "It's on." He would think about the whole River thing later. After Tink got through beating the crap out of him.

His world narrowed to strikes and parries, punches and chops, kicks and sweeps. He barely felt the blows that got past him and he thought he'd even landed a few good ones himself. He was still raring to go when Tink called a halt by stepping back after her latest pass, her feet leaving the mat entirely.

"That's more like it," she told him, sounding pleased. Or as pleased as Tink ever did, which wasn't much. Hell, she'd done a demo with Marcus once during which he'd taken her down hard enough that Tink had literally lain on the mat for nearly two minutes. When she'd rolled to her feet after a few long, hard breaths, her only comment had been, "Good one. Now try it again." The second attempt hadn't gone so well for her opponent.

"I'll do better next time," Morgan answered as he backed away, stepping onto cement and grabbing the towel he'd brought with him. "I'm just...distracted.

But you're right, Tink. I need to be *here* when I'm here."

Tink nodded as Morgan wiped sweat from his chest, and fuck him, but she wasn't even breathing hard. Christ. "You do. But you came back well, and you're not usually so...off. Is everything all right?" And that was the other thing about Tink. When she wasn't kicking someone's ass on the mat, she was one of the nicest people Morgan had ever met. She cared about each and every Gentleman and Lady she trained, which meant the entire Club's roster of actives.

Even so, they were friendly but not exactly friends. They didn't meet up for lunch or shoot the shit. And there was about zero chance of Morgan telling Tink what he'd been distracted by. So "Yeah," he said with a grin, rubbing the towel over his sweat-damp hair. "Just something with one of my team. No big deal." Because it wasn't. Or not to anyone who wasn't him or Simon.

Or River, Morgan reminded himself as he headed back towards his rooms, limping slightly. Then again, River might not think it was a big deal at all, considering how much the kid fucked around. And it wasn't, really, Morgan was sure. It was just sex. Fucking. Even though he and Simon hadn't ever wanted someone enough to matter, Morgan was damned sure that they wanted River that much. And Simon had said...yeah. Sun and naked skin and tight heat. River coming right there, then just saying okay, he was on board with getting sweaty and worn out with Simon and Morgan.

It was an exciting thought. Morgan had to admit that. River was fucking stunning. The idea of what Simon had described was fucking amazing. Fucking River. Simon fucking River. Mouths and hands and…Jesus fucking Christ, Morgan would have been embarrassed about the wood he was suddenly sporting if he hadn't still had his towel.

He spent a few minutes exchanging what passed for pleasantries with a couple of Gentlemen in the elevator; just "Have you tried the new semi-auto since Franz retooled it?" and "Hook's team took out a whole fucking nest of Blackhearts last week." The usual, really.

It helped. Helped a lot. Morgan even felt fine about draping the towel around his neck by the time he reached his floor. Then he headed off down the corridor with a wave for the guys still riding and he was fine. He needed a shower, but yeah. He was fine. Right up until he turned the corner towards the rooms he shared with Simon and Rico. Then his not so little problem came back with a vengeance and he moaned, a stuttered step letting him stop.

"Dude. What's up?" Fuck if River wasn't grinning. Grinning and giving him a long look, Morgan realised, though the man's blue eyes seemed to get stuck on the front of Morgan's sweats.

The heat in his cheeks meant he was blushing, Morgan knew. Blushing and staring. "I thought you were topside for two more days," he heard himself saying and River shrugged. Stayed right there next to Morgan's door.

"I wanted to talk to you," River answered. "You know…make sure Simon had all his shit right." Those eyes darted up to Morgan's, and fuck if River didn't wink. "Looks like he did, man. Cool. You planning on standing there all day?"

Well, that was the fucking question, wasn't it? Answered pretty damned easily, but still. "No," Morgan said, feet finally starting to move again. "Just surprised to see you, Riv. So how's the...I mean, how are things up at the Ranch?"

River grinned even more and there was something so fucking knowing in the kid's eyes, Morgan wanted to snarl. He didn't, but he wanted to. "You know that little lake that's almost off the Ranch grounds?" River asked instead of answering. "There's a house there. I found it yesterday. Doesn't look like anyone's been there for a while, though."

"Okay, and I care...why?" Morgan demanded, and sure, he sounded a little gruff, even to himself, but fuck it. Between his fucking cock and being surprised that River wasn't still above, he figured gruff was reasonable.

River shrugged again, like he wasn't even a little bit freaked out by Morgan's obvious hard-on. And maybe he wasn't, Morgan realised when he gave the kid a quick up and down glance of his own. Maybe Morgan's cock being hard wasn't an issue because River's for damned sure was too, though it didn't seem to be affecting the kid's ability to speak any.

"I just thought it was kind of sad," River said then, and yeah. His voice was the same as always. Not even a little bit rough. Christ. "So are you gonna invite me in, man, or do you want me to attack you out here?"

Morgan blinked, trying to catch up with the conversation, with the way River had just gone from talking about some shack to... Well, to a statement of intent that Morgan couldn't really object to. Fuck, the kid was cool. Calm, damn it. Like the idea of touching Morgan, or whatever the fuck River had in mind, was just another thing. Fuck, he wanted to make River lose that unexpected poise. And Simon was out, picking some shit up in town. Rico was getting another computer hacking lesson from Jensen, the Club's security guy. Their rooms were empty.

Keycard, then palm print. Then, "Get your fucking ass inside," when the door opened. And River was still grinning, those eyes were still bright blue and giving Morgan that look, like River knew exactly what he was thinking. Then the door closed behind them and Morgan flipped the manual lock, and maybe River wasn't as unaffected as he'd seemed because that lithe body was up against him, pressing Morgan to the door, and there were blue eyes becoming more pupil than anything else just a few inches from Morgan's own.

"Simon didn't mention if you guys like to kiss," River muttered, his voice lower, all of a sudden. Deeper, but still so damned smooth.

"Find out." Morgan grunted, breath pushed from him as River pressed harder against him, that pretty fucking mouth right there on his, lips open, soft but insistent, tongue sliding in when Morgan gave it the chance, and it was good. Fucking good. Christ.

Maybe too good, to be standing there letting River have his way. Shit, it was hot, though. Hot and fucking…something. Wrong, maybe. Wrong to be there with River, without Simon. Because somehow, for whatever reason, it sort of felt like cheating, Morgan realised. No matter what he and Simon had talked about, being there, in his and Simon's rooms, alone with River, felt good and hot and borderline primal…and wrong.

Fuck if pushing River away wasn't the hardest damned thing Morgan had done in months, but he had to, he figured. If he wanted to be able to look Simon in the eyes ever again, he had to…not stop things, but just postpone them.

Morgan was breathing hard by the time he made his hands listen to his brain. Harder, more like. Even so, he leaned against the door, his hands on River's shoulders holding the blond almost at arm's length. "Is that what you wanted to know?" Morgan asked, and if his voice was still rough and a little bit raw, he figured that was fine. Hell, River looked just as shaky, just as jagged as Morgan felt. River grinned, though, just like that.

One hand reached towards him and Morgan groaned deeply as River brushed the front of his tented sweats, just the vaguest, lightest touch of fingers that had Morgan's cock begging for more. "Fuck."

"Soon," River answered, sounding agreeable, for fuck's sake, but yeah. A little harsh edge there, too. It actually helped Morgan to feel less like a lecherous prick. "Okay." Fuck if the kid wasn't stepping back, like they hadn't been humping at the fucking door just moments earlier. "Okay," again, River's eyes fucking dancing. "I'll be back in my rooms right on schedule, man. You and Simon decide to pay me a visit, you know where I am."

Morgan was still blinking when River pushed him away from the door to flip the toggle lock. Then the door was open and River grinned even more. Probably at the fucking baffled look on his face, Morgan realised. "Uh, okay. We will. I mean, we..."

The kid laughed. He fucking laughed. "You will, dude. I know. 'S cool." Those blue eyes raked down Morgan's body again, like a touch or a breeze or something more than a fucking gaze should be. "You know, Simon's right, Morgan," River said, standing there in the doorway, one hand on the jamb. "You're gonna split me in half with your fucking cock." He grinned while Morgan groaned. "Looking forward to it, man." Then River was gone and the door was closing and Morgan was glad. He didn't have a fucking clue what he could have said to that.

"Shit." Except for that.

* * * *

He still had it, River thought smugly, even as he packed for his trip below. It took maybe five seconds, considering all he'd actually brought up to the Ranch was the scrub pants he'd been wearing when he'd left Med and a single change of clothes, which he was wearing.

The rest was nothing more than a bottle of coconut and pineapple scented tanning oil, which some insisted on calling pinà colada, a few hair ties, a couple of books, toiletries, and his hair brush. It fit easily into the small tie-dyed backpack he'd grabbed from his rooms two days earlier, after he'd talked to Morgan.

A broad grin spread his lips as he shouldered the pack because it wasn't exactly a lie. They'd talked, he and Morgan, just...not a lot. Enough to know they were on the same page, which was really the part that mattered.

Morgan's mouth had been nice, though. Nicer when it wasn't spitting words, even if the growly tone Morgan had been using went straight to River's balls. Yeah, growly was awesome, River decided, still grinning as he stepped from the bunk house and made his way across the grass and dirt and gravel to Marcus and Tanner's place.

He didn't have to knock. The house was never locked during the day, but it was just polite to give a little warning. He wouldn't want to walk in on the guys fucking, because that would be just horrible, River thought with a silent laugh that faded quickly. Huh. He actually didn't want to see that. Weird.

"It's open," he heard, so River shook it off and opened the door. Tanner, looking just as fucking gorgeous as always, stood in the living room off to the left and just looked at him for a minute. Then the redhead nodded just a little. "Time to go down?"

"You have no idea," River heard himself saying before he could stop himself, but screw it. He'd been messing with Tanner for two weeks. What was one little comment? "Not training today?" Because Tanner was usually either below or out on the extended grounds putting the Alt teams through their paces. Since taking over the training of the Alternate teams who handled the special Games for FGC, he hadn't lost a Gentleman or Lady, so Tanner was obviously damned good at it.

A red brow arched, green eyes giving River a sharp look that he couldn't miss. "I thought someone should be here to see you off and Marcus is working today."

River shrugged and hitched the strap of his backpack higher onto his shoulder. "Whatever, man. I figured you'd both be out. I was gonna leave a note to say thanks. I know it was probably driving you guys nuts. In the bad way. You know, the naked and shit." He shrugged again. "My ass is all better, so it and I both thank you." He winked and Tanner laughed, like maybe he couldn't believe River had said that.

"Well, let's just get you on your way, River." That was what Tanner said, but the guy sounded strange. Like there was more. So River crossed his arms and closed the front door, then moved to stand in the living room doorway, leaning against the moulding.

"And?" he prodded. Carefully, because he liked Tanner but River hadn't quite figured the guy out. Some days he was like a buddy; others Tanner acted like River had said something to offend him. He was never quite sure which Tanner he would get. He did know Tanner's changing attitudes were specific to *him*, though. River was the only one who got that mercurial side.

Tanner sighed and cocked his head, and River just stood there. It looked like the dude was thinking. "You get hurt a lot," Tanner finally said. "Then you come to the Ranch. Almost every Game, you end up here, after."

Was that all? River grinned. "You guys have the sky up here, man. Horses. Grass. Fucking nature. And I lived most of my life in the desert. Arizona, you know? So maybe I'm not super hyped about living in a fucking cave underground all the time." And River didn't get hurt on purpose. Maybe he let his guard down sometimes, at the end of a Game, but it wasn't deliberate. Tanner seemed to think otherwise, though. Shit. If Tanner reported anything like that to the Events Coordinator, Tanner's sister Patrice, who was also Assistant Director of the whole FGC, River would probably find himself ordered to stay underground every minute when he wasn't actively Playing.

"And that's all it is. Just...missing the outdoors." Not a question, so River didn't answer. "It doesn't have anything to do with seeing Marcus."

River snorted. "Fuck, man. He's never even up here during the day, and I'm always in the bunk house after dark. I'd see him more down below." It was true, too. River wasn't a big fan of the dark. Never had been. Inside with the lights on at night suited him just fine.

For whatever reason, his words seemed to satisfy Tanner because the dude grinned back at him. River shrugged, then shifted from foot to foot. "So, we done here, man? I should get going."

That fucking brow again. "You're in a hurry to leave 'the sky and shit,' all of a sudden?"

Another snort left River and he had a feeling he was blushing just a little. "More like I'm in a hurry to get down to my rooms and get naked, dude. I have a…fuck. A date, I guess. Come on, Tanner, I've been up here for weeks. I really need to get laid." Repeatedly, if he was lucky.

Tanner's grin got wider, and just like that the man was ushering River to the elevator. "Well, whoever it is, undo your hair, Riv. It's a huge turn-on. Whoever you're with will love it."

River laughed softly. "Most guys around here do, man, but I haven't really asked them. They could have a thing for short, but who knows?" Then he stepped into the elevator and laughed again when he saw Tanner mouthing '*Them?*' as the doors closed.

Chapter Five

"What's wrong, love?" It was a good question, Simon decided, because while even the day before Morgan had been nearly vibrating at the thought of what they planned to do with River, now that the day had arrived Morgan was tense. A wee bit growly, though not in the usual, fun way. "Talk to me, yeah?"

Always a tough one, getting Morgan to share his feelings. Of course, Simon wasn't rightly the talk-it-to-death type himself, but he generally had the decency to give his bloke a bloody clue. Morgan, though...well, with Morgan it was like pulling teeth, more often than not.

Simon smiled and dragged off his shirt, tossing it in the general direction of the corner, where it would likely mate with the small pile of other sweat-stained garments until either he or his bloke decided to drop them with the cleaning staff. "Come on. Tell Si what's rattling about in that pretty head of yours."

Morgan gave him a glare that only made Simon smirk. The bloke always did that when Simon even suggested prettiness on Morgan's side. Simon couldn't really blame him, though. Morgan wasn't pretty. Bloody well stunning, yeah, but pretty? Too much man and muscle to be strictly pretty. Even when Morgan was sitting on the edge of their bed and clearly pouting under the glares and snarls. Pouting and looking a bit worried, even, though Simon figured no one else would have noticed. Nobody knew Morgan like Simon did, though. Except Jericho, but she knew *everyone* far better than most knew or would like to find out.

"Right, then." Simon frowned slightly as he shimmied out of his pants and kicked them after his shirt, and Morgan didn't even look at what was revealed. Bloody hell. Morgan just kept glaring, eyes locked on Simon's, and yeah. That was definitely a good degree of uncertainty in Morgan's eyes.

Fortunately, Simon knew exactly how to get his bloke talking, even with the mood Morgan was in. It wasn't often that Simon's love went through moments of self-doubt, but it happened; usually when Morgan was about to step out of his comfort zones. Or when he was remembering what had happened while retrieving Jericho following her abduction by the wretched twat who'd been experimenting on her and other kids in NovoTech's underground complex, Simon recalled. This? Well, this could be either. Same remedy, thank bloody Christ.

He crossed the floor, carpet soft under his bare feet, and when he reached Morgan he just stood there for a moment in front of tanned skin and muscle and soft brown hair. Then Simon snorted and pushed Morgan back, down onto their bed, the bloke's long, denim-clad legs still stretching from mattress to floor. He grinned as he settled himself on Morgan's body, straddling his solid waist. He rested his hands on Morgan's shoulders as he met Morgan's deep brown eyes. Deep, annoyed, but also slightly amused brown eyes.

"It's been a long day, love" — Simon began — "and I know you were fine this morning. Showed me as much in the shower, yeah? So, seems like sometime between leaving this room and coming back, somebody pissed in your bloody porridge. Now, you're going to tell me what's bashing about in your brain and making you act the git. Then we'll be having another shower. Eventually."

Morgan sighed softly, the mulish cast that had still been colouring his features fading. His long, strong arms rose and Simon felt thick fingers on his sides, his back, moving over his skin until they finally settled on Simon's hips. "It's stupid," Morgan muttered then, like he was ashamed, and Simon groaned silently. "I even know it's stupid, okay? So just…it's nothing, Si."

Simon snorted again. "Bloody well *something*, love, if it's got you thinking anything about you's stupid. Daft bugger. So, what then? Is it River? Know you were looking forward to seeing him tonight. Changed your mind?" The twitch of Morgan's cock under Simon's body and Morgan's trousers seemed to disagree with the suggestion, though. The sudden shamed look that crossed Morgan's face almost too quickly to see presented another notion. One Simon was entirely familiar with and hated with a fiery passion.

"Oh, bloody hell." He frowned, then leant down and kissed Morgan hard, rough. Lips and teeth, tongue driving deep. Simon took every minuscule dip and whorl in his bloke's mouth with intent, mapping the familiar territory with determined force. He was hard against Morgan when he pulled back, but Morgan was doing far more than twitch in those jeans, Simon noted with a smirk. "Right. Let's make this clear as crystal, love. You. Are mine. Not dirty, not ruined, not anything but what I say you are, and that's fine and strong and right. Bastard what touched you is dead and gone, over a year under a great pile of rubble, yeah?"

Morgan nodded slowly, though there was still a bit of that sickened fear in his eyes. Simon would never call it fear to Morgan's face, but it was, and he bloody well knew it. Had seen it in the mirror a few times in his younger days. "I know," Morgan said quietly, blushing just a bit. "I told you it was stupid. I just...what if...Christ, I don't know."

Arched brows met Morgan's words and Simon kissed those full red lips again, though more softly than before. "What if? What if...what, love?" Because they were finally getting somewhere. Bloody hell. Pulling teeth, indeed.

A long, deep breath, then Morgan exhaled and took another. He bit his lip and Simon stroked one hand up from Morgan's shoulder to cup a stubbled cheek. "What if he can tell, Simon?" Morgan whispered the words, eyes closed. "What if River can tell? I...you love me, so you get it, but he's not...he's not you and he doesn't, and what if..."

Bloody hell. Simon shook his head, even while he ruthlessly buried the part of him that wanted to slap Morgan for not just getting the bloody fuck over it and going on with his life. Their life. "What if we just tell him, love?" was what Simon finally said, though only a few moments had passed. "If you're that bloody concerned over it, could just put it out there, yeah?"

It was exactly what they should do, Simon realised. Even though Morgan looked scandalised and a good bit fearful, it was a worthwhile notion. They liked River. They for damned sure wanted the bloke. And River wasn't the sort to give credence to any rubbish like Morgan being stained by something he couldn't have avoided even had he not been drugged unconscious. Morgan had still been bound; helpless. The drugs just meant he didn't remember it, but for what the prat who'd done the deed had told him. Sexual abuse, be it with cock or just fingers, as the bastard had done to Morgan, wasn't the fault of the victim. Simon was reasonably sure that River was bright enough to know as much, too. Even though Morgan still had moments during which he thought of himself as dirty for 'letting' it happen, Simon thought River would know better. Just as Morgan did most of the time. "Think that's the answer, love. We just tell him."

Morgan didn't look happy with the idea, but then Simon hadn't expected him to be. Even so, Simon hushed his bloke's objections with another kiss. They would do it. Then Morgan would see. Understand that Simon wasn't ignoring what had happened out of love, but that it truly didn't matter. That some prat with grabby hands truly didn't make Morgan dirty. Yeah.

"Come on, love," Simon murmured against Morgan's soft, kiss-wet lips. "Time for that shower, yeah? Patrice says Petal can stay with her till we're home, though I hate subjecting our girl to the bint more than necessary." Petal, aka Princess, aka Jericho, aka Rico seemed to enjoy his nicknames for her, and as everyone knew who he meant when using the first two, Simon had no plan to stop. Just as he intended to continue calling Patrice whatever struck his fancy.

He'd likely use harpy again soon, rather than bint for a change.

That reference had Morgan laughing, just like Simon had hoped. It wasn't a full laugh, not yet, but it was good. Meant Morgan was pulling out of his funk. "Rico likes Patrice," Morgan reminded him and Simon made a face as he shifted, slid back, stood.

"Yeah, well," Simon smirked as he held out one hand, "Jericho's a lot of things, love. Beautiful little chit, smart and bloody well frightening, most days. Doesn't mean she's got a lick of sense when it comes to people, does it?" He winked and pulled Morgan to his feet when that big, warm hand took his. "Rather question her taste in general, actually," he added as he started for the bathroom, with Morgan right behind him. "Have you *seen* the bloody shoes she's collected on her wish list? More suited to a street walker...or the viscous, nasty twat herself." By which, of course, Simon meant Patrice. He had many terms for her. Bint and twat were among the nicer ones. They had a friendly but still antagonistic relationship, most days.

Simon winked as he started the shower running, his other hand still holding Morgan's, and this time Morgan's laugh was better. Stronger. His bloke always did bounce back well.

"You almost sound like you don't like Patrice," Morgan answered as he let go of Simon to push jeans down long, strong legs. Yeah. Hard, all right. Good. "Lucky I know better or I'd be worried about leaving Rico with her."

Simon chuckled as he stepped into the shower and made room for Morgan behind him. "That's our little secret, love," he murmured as Morgan closed the shower door. "Keep it to yourself or bloody Patrice will start thinking I'll go easy on her. Now, enough talk about bitchy-bitch, yeah? Got better things for us to do with our mouths."

* * * *

Simon's words and reassurances aside, the last thing Morgan was expecting when he stammered out the truth of what had happened to him in that underground labyrinth of horrors was for River to frown and hug him, right there in River's living room. That was what he got, sure, but it was damned unexpected.

"That sucks ass, man," River said against Morgan's ear. "Not the good kind, either." Then River stepped back and Simon had that told-you-so right there on his face and Morgan rolled his eyes.

"Fine," Morgan grumbled, giving Simon what he knew had to be an embarrassed gaze. "I told you before, Si. I knew it was stupid."

Another few minutes while River pointed them to the couch and got some beers, Simon explaining a little about what Morgan had been thinking before, and Morgan was blushing. He knew he was fucking blushing. He could feel it as heat in his cheeks, for fuck's sake.

"Whoa. Harsh." River was shaking his head, but he was smiling a little, too. "Morgan. Man." Another head shake. "Seriously, that whole thing was fucked up. It sort of explains why you totally looked like shit when you guys came back to the Hummers, though. I figured it was 'cause of Jericho, but yeah. Wow."

And River had been there. River and Moon. Morgan had forgotten that part, but that mission was when Simon had met the Stones, after Morgan had been...taken. Tricked and dragged off against his will.

It was sort of comforting, in a weird way. Even with all the Games he'd Played in on the same team with River, knowing Riv had been there back then…helped.

Morgan shrugged, the heat in his face fading just a bit as he sipped his beer. Corona wasn't his favourite, but it would do. "Simon's right," he said after a long swallow. "I even know he's right, okay? And I do want you, Riv. We both do. Maybe more than you know. But it's…fuck if I can explain it."

Simon chuckled a little and then his hand was on Morgan's thigh and it was okay, suddenly. Better. Like Simon was his anchor, Morgan decided. And maybe Simon was, in ways Morgan had never really considered. Oh, he'd known he felt safe and settled with Simon, like the man somehow made him better and more. He hadn't been consciously aware that Simon could soothe him with a touch, though. It was pretty fucking cool and not at all scary, which was a little bit surprising but not a bad thing. Not a bad thing at all.

Simon gave him a nod, seemingly an encouraging gesture, but the Brit seemed fine with letting Morgan have his say because that soft mouth was staying closed except for frequent sips of beer. It was strange, having Simon silent. Simon usually had more fucking shit to say than anyone Morgan had ever known. But it was a sign of…something. Trust or love or…Morgan didn't know what, but there were a crazy amount of emotions in Simon's eyes; he did know that much.

"I guess I'm…" Morgan started, but he trailed off, not sure of how to put it into words without sounding like a fucking idiot.

"Kind of freaked out, man," River finished for him with a grin, tipping a half-empty bottle of Corona at him from just a few feet away. "Makes sense, you know? I mean, think about it. Some crazy fucking bitch had you kidnapped, and some sick bastard got off on telling you what he did to you while you were out like a fucking light. Then you made it worse—for yourself, I mean—by getting away all on your own."

River nodded sharply, like it was the most obvious thing in the world, even though Morgan didn't get it. "Huh?" And Simon's hand was suddenly hard, digging in to Morgan's thigh. Not painfully, but still way more than just resting there all of a fucking sudden.

Another swallow of beer and River shrugged. "I'm just saying, man. You got yourself out of there, right? So some part of you, like...deep down inside...probably feels like you should have been able to get the fuck away before he even touched you. And you didn't, so that same crazy, primitive part thinks you probably enjoyed it or deserved it or some shit like that." Another shrug. "Lizard-mind, man. Doesn't always make sense, but it's there, you know?"

Just like that, Simon was up from the couch and in front of River. Morgan had barely even seen him move, his mind was whirring so much. He'd felt that hand leave his thigh, though. Its absence was a cold spot on his leg.

"Bright boy, aren't you, mate?" Morgan heard Simon say, then Simon was kissing River and Morgan wasn't paying attention to his racing brain any more. He was too busy watching his lover and River pressed tight together, free hands touching each other while the hands holding beer threatened to tip pale golden liquid all over the floor.

Morgan figured he should be jealous, but God they looked good together. Brown hair, short and soft, and blond, long and smooth-looking even in the braid River always wore. So fucking hot to see them like that. And he wasn't jealous. Not at all, though when he spared a brief moment to consider seeing Simon that way with anyone other than River? Oh, yeah. Hot and sour and bitter, right there in his chest.

And maybe River was right, Morgan realised. Maybe he was punishing himself for something he knew, intellectually, wasn't his fault. The idea would take some time to sink in, he was sure, but if River was right, then it would. It would sink in, soak into his psyche, and...yeah.

"You planning to sit there all night, love?" Simon asked, and he sounded so amused but still aroused. So fucking demanding, too. He hadn't let go of River, but Simon wasn't kissing him anymore, he was looking at Morgan. He started to reach out and Morgan saw the moment Simon noticed there was still a beer bottle in his hand. Then Simon and River both laughed, and Morgan found himself chuckling too.

"I don't know," Morgan answered, the welcome amusement easing whatever small bit of reticence had been left in him. "I'm kind of liking the show, Si. Hell, I'm about halfway there just from seeing that fucking kiss." It was true, too. His slacks were getting tight, his cock filling from the small, wet sounds he'd heard and the way Simon and River had looked, mouths pressed tightly together.

Simon arched a brow at him—so simple, so clearly implying Morgan was out of his mind that Morgan laughed again. "Sod watching, love. Haul your gorgeous ass up off that couch and get it over here, yeah?"

"Bring the rest of you too, man," River added, and Morgan couldn't do anything but nod, stand, and move to them.

"You're gonna make a mess, guys," he said quickly, even though his body was humming.

"Bloody well hope so," Simon agreed, but River grinned and shook his head.

"He means the beer, man," and Morgan did, so he didn't bother saying anything to River then. He just took the bottles from Simon and River and set them beside his own on the table in front of the couch.

Morgan raised his arms slowly, one wrapping easily around Simon, the other circling River's waist more tentatively. "So, um. How do we...do this?" Okay, he felt a little stupid, but he really didn't know. The fucking logistics of three guys hadn't really occurred to him when he and Simon had decided to give the whole thing with River a shot. Christ, he was...whatever. Confused. A little bit lost, even. Then Morgan felt River's hand on the back of his neck and River was kissing him and Morgan stopped wondering, stopped worrying. He just let it happen at first, until Simon plastered himself up against them, hands Morgan knew almost as well as his own touching, stroking, and it was good.

Simon pushed in, took over the kiss from River, and Morgan moaned softly, letting Simon in, taking Simon's tongue without any of the embarrassment he'd somehow expected at having River see them. Then, again, River was right there in their clench, pushing in, the tip of his tongue sliding a soft, wet track where Morgan's mouth met Simon's, and yeah. Okay. Fucking good, and not embarrassing at all. It seemed right, somehow.

Morgan felt his feet moving, though he wasn't paying much attention to that part of his body. He was fully consumed by mouths and hands and sensations that threatened to overwhelm him already and they were still dressed, for fuck's sake. Still standing and touching and…and River pulled away, then Morgan was blind for just a second as his shirt covered his face before disappearing to wherever shirts went in that sort of situation. Somewhere that wasn't on his body, in any case, and that was what mattered.

More movement, more skin, more kisses that Morgan felt all the way down to his gut, to his balls. Simon's lips on his chest, teeth scraping just right over Morgan's nipples, first one, then the other. And silk, long strands of pure silk that smelt like sandalwood and pine, which proved to be River's hair, unbound somehow during the momentary eternity they'd already enjoyed, and it wasn't anywhere near over. Hell, they'd barely even begun.

Chapter Six

Morgan wasn't sure when he'd kicked off his shoes, or even when they'd left the living room, but there was carpeting under his feet, feeling like some unlikely cross between industrial and luxurious, and Simon was still tormenting his chest. Still laving and biting and pulling gasps from Morgan that he didn't even know he was releasing until he heard them on the air. Then River stepped away, was at Morgan's back, hands moving, lips on Morgan's shoulder, skin rubbing skin and it was too much. Too much and not enough.

"Oh, hell," Morgan heard, his own voice and so rough, raw, so low and grating. Christ. Fucking Christ. "Shit, don't..."

"Bed, love." Simon groaned the words, the small vibrations singing through Morgan's flesh, and somewhere between the words and the sensation of falling, of landing on soft sheets, Morgan's pants ended up around his ankles, then on the floor.

"Dude." River, though Morgan couldn't see him. Couldn't see anything with his eyes closed, but he couldn't open them. Couldn't look and see Simon and River standing, still partly dressed while Morgan was naked and on display. It was too...something. "Dude," River said again and the mattress dipped beside Morgan, a warm, slightly damp hand suddenly resting on his stomach. "You're so damn hot, man."

A chuckle from Simon, full of what sounded like some sort of smug pride, and another dip to the bed beneath Morgan as Simon joined them. Another hand, just as warm, less moist but Morgan knew that hand. "My bloke's a bloody stunner, mate," Simon said easily. "Knew that much as soon as I saw him."

Mouths again, on him, on his skin. Hands and fingers, stroking, rubbing, caressing abs and sides and hip bones, moving closer, closer to Morgan's centre, his prick. "Oh...oh, fuck," he moaned, trying not to move though it was impossible. And River, because Morgan could feel that long-ass hair move, was licking a path down, flicking his tongue in Morgan's navel and Morgan couldn't help touching, fisting his hand in hair.

Long, silky strands slid between his fingers, his other hand hard on Simon's back. "Oh, fuck." Again, because Morgan couldn't seem to say anything else. His senses were full, wrapped in the touch of his lover and their...whatever the fuck River was to them. More than friend and fellow Gentleman, that much Morgan knew, but less than lover or boyfriend; that much was clear, too. Whatever the word was, it didn't matter. The whole thing was overwhelming. Not better than being with Simon alone, but different.

Hard cocks, just as hard as his own, pressed against Morgan's legs. Small, slick bits of fluid painted his skin. Simon felt right against him, felt like everything Morgan had ever needed. And River…Christ. River. Hot and slick, River's prick felt long though not thick. Like the man himself, Morgan thought with a bit of amusement that didn't make it to his lips. And that was just as well because Simon was there, lips on Morgan's, kissing him hard, strong, possessing Morgan's mouth with the taste of Morgan's skin and River's kiss right there on his tongue.

"Oh, man," River again, pulling away from Morgan's stomach. "Shit, you two are fucking awesome. I mean, yeah. Knew that. Duh. But damn, dudes. I need to get the rubbers. Be right back."

"You all right, love?" Simon murmured against his lips and Morgan finally—finally—opened his eyes to meet his lover's heated but slightly concerned greyish blue stare.

He nodded a little, but Morgan knew Simon saw it. Simon always saw. Even when Morgan didn't want him to, but it wasn't one of those times. "Yeah," Morgan whispered back, his hand moving on Simon, on skin he knew and loved more than he'd ever been able to say. "I. It's a lot. But yeah. I'm good. Fucking great, I think."

Saying it actually seemed to make it so because Morgan felt something inside him relaxing, then letting go completely when Simon pulled back a little and grinned, pleasure clear in those pretty eyes. "Good, love," Simon answered with a tiny smirk that had Morgan's body tingling all over. Or tingling more, because Christ he was keyed up. "Can't wait to see your face when our boy climbs on and rides your bloody brilliant cock home, yeah?"

Fuck. Hell, yes. The idea of it, of being buried in River's ass from below—the same ass Simon had said was so fucking tight around just one finger—was enough to have his balls throbbing. Enough to have them pushing one short but heavy gush of slick fluid from Morgan's dick. "Christ, Si."

He might have said more, but River was back. Standing at the end of the bed, little plastic bag in hand, River wasn't staring exactly. He was darting his gaze up and down the both of them, Morgan noticed. Taking them in and liking what he saw because River's cock was sort of bouncing just a little. It was amazing. No, River wasn't staring, but Morgan was. He couldn't help it.

Golden skin. Not dark and brown like Morgan got when he was truly tanned, but fucking golden. Shit. Golden and smooth, no hair on River's chest unless it was so light it was invisible. Small copper nipples, tight and hard, pointed right at him, at Simon. Enough muscle that River's ribs were a suggestion, rather than an announcement. Abdomen, toned but not overly defined. Cobbles hinted at more than anything else. Hip bones sharply visible, in the best possible way, and those little divots Simon had, too. Just small indentations Morgan wanted to press his tongue into, scrape with his teeth.

And fuck, he'd been right, Morgan saw, when he finally let himself gaze at the proud flesh jutting from River's groin. Long and thin and bent slightly to the left. Golden too, but darker, pinker, closer to bronze, though that was likely from the blood gathered there. Small tracks of wetness trailing down the length, shimmering in the lamplight from beside the bed, and yeah. Yeah, he could so fucking do that. Have River ride him.

"Fuck, you're hot, Riv," Morgan said then, and it was just a fact. Blunt. Plainly stated. Obvious. "Christ."

River laughed, his head dropping back to let the sound rise to the ceiling. "Man, you read my mind. About you guys." Then one of those blue-blue eyes winked and River was on the bed again, still holding that bag. Holding it up, really, like it was a fucking prize. "So who wants to do the honours?" River asked, his smile wide and easy. "If I'm gonna ride Morgan's big fat cock, I'll need to be plenty slick. I'd do it myself but I think I'll be busy."

Then River was leaning over him and his lips were on Morgan's yet again and yeah. Okay. The bag really was a prize. Of course, so was River. Enough so that Morgan could only groan his agreement into River's mouth at Simon's chuckled, "Only right to ride my fingers before you ride my bloke, mate." Simon moved, and Morgan missed his lover's warmth against him, but it was fine. Simon wasn't really going anywhere.

One hand in River's hair, holding the guy's head close and angled just right for Morgan's liking. The other hand sliding down River's spine, teasing the top of the toned, rounded ass Morgan so wanted inside of. And River's leg, thrown over Morgan's thighs, sudden moans and groans feeding into him as River started to shift, to rock as Simon clearly did as he'd promised. Morgan slid his hand down farther, the kiss going deeper when he felt Simon's fingers, digits slippery and warm, pushing in, pulling out of River's body.

It was weird and hot and felt sort of dirty, but in the good way. The oh-fuck-this-is-amazing way. And River's leg hitched higher, one knee pushing right up against Morgan's sac and that was good, too. Almost *too* good, but not…quite. And all the while, River was kissing Morgan, lips hot and fierce, tongue jabbing and swirling in what Morgan noticed was an echo of Simon's fingers, and that made it even better. Like they really were all in it together, one unit working towards the same goal.

"Enough," River grunted, mouth leaving Morgan's open and still wanting. "Fuck, Simon, that's enough. Bag. Need one of the extra-large to cover this big dog, man."

Simon must have taken care of it because River for damned sure didn't move, but seconds later, after the sound of tearing plastic, River's hand was there, somehow holding Morgan's cock still while rolling slick, tight latex over him and damn if Morgan wasn't aching. Aching and fucking desperate. "Fuck. Riv. Christ."

"Oh, man. You're gonna fill me right up, Morgan. Shit. Look at that thing." River was grinning again, looking dazed and maybe a little bit stoned, but grinning. Then he moved, sliding over Morgan, getting to his knees, shifting upwards, and Morgan moaned.

He heard Simon laughing, and even that sounded smug. Then Simon spoke, and yeah. Smug was the word. "Word of advice, mate." Mate. Talking to River, then. Good. Morgan wouldn't have been able to answer anyway. "Put your hands on his chest, yeah? Then just push back. I'll hold him steady till you've a good start." Which only made sense when Morgan felt Simon's hand wrapped around his dick, keeping it pointed where it seemed to be needed.

Oh, fuck. Yeah. Fuck yeah. Strange with the condom. Less heat. Less immediate sensation. But that was good, Morgan thought blearily as River moved again and Morgan felt pressure, warmth against his tip. And Simon... Christ, Simon was jacking him, just a little, just gently, while River pushed, dropped maybe half an inch, blue eyes staring into Morgan's and going wide.

"Fucking awesome," River murmured, the sound like a purr, like velvet as he rocked left and right, back and forth, then pushed down again. "Oh, man. Yeah, that's fucking good, man. Just like...yeah. Like that."

One more shimmy and shove and fuck if Morgan didn't yelp a little when he felt his tip surrounded, taken in. But River was whimpering too, so it was fine, and Simon. Oh, Christ, Simon was stroking him, pushing his hand up Morgan's shaft to where it disappeared inside River's body. Simon touched, rubbed lightly, and it was filthy, perfect. Right. "Si...shit, Si. Gonna make me come..."

River nodded, bottom lip between his teeth for a second. "Yeah, Simon. Stop it, man. It's too fucking much." And River pushed down again, started a slow slide to Morgan's base that had both of them wide-eyed and staring while Simon grumbled and moved away.

"Right, then," Simon was beside them, just like that, lying on his side and smirking yet again. Fuck, maybe Simon always smirked while fucking and Morgan had just never noticed. "Better view from here anyway." Then Simon leant in and his mouth was on Morgan's nipple between River's fingers, though Morgan could tell he was watching the way River was taking Morgan in.

Fuck. So much heat. Pressure. River was just as tight as Simon had said. Just as tight as Simon still was, even after more than a year. Tight and hot, even with the latex, and Christ. Christ.

"All the way, pet," Simon groaned the words, cheek on Morgan's shoulder, breath cool on Morgan's sweat-damp skin. "Let me see it, River. One long drop, yeah?"

River's laugh sounded breathless. "You don't ask much, do you, man?"

"Fucking...demanding...bastard," Morgan heard himself moan, but Simon just laughed at the truth of it. Then River did it. Just took a breath and took Morgan in to the hilt as that same breath shuddered past River's lips on the way out. "Christ!"

"Fucking...awesome!" A cry, River's eyes on the ceiling, head arched back, long blond hair trailing on Morgan's thighs. And Simon was stroking himself. Morgan could feel his knuckles against his skin, feel the bed shift ever so slightly, he and River were so still. "Fuck, it's like riding a telephone pole," River gasped out, like the words barely fit inside and needed to leave him to make room.

Simon chuckled, though Morgan could hear the little hitch there. Hear how turned on Simon was, though the increased speed of the knuckles against him told him as much, too. "Not precisely riding, are you, pet? More like sitting at the moment. Want to see you bloody well move." Yeah, demanding fucking bastard was right. "Nothing quite like the first time, mate. Riding that hot bloody cock. Pushes in, holds your bum so wide, feels impossible to believe it even fits, yeah?" Another chuckle and Simon's hand left his own cock because it was suddenly right there on River's, and Christ that looked incredible.

Felt it, too, Morgan figured, because River grunted, looking down, and he shifted a little, rocking forward and back, just enough to have Morgan gasping and fastening his hands hard on River's hips to keep that small movement going. "Never stops feeling like a great sodding bludgeon inside you, either," Simon went on, fingers barely brushing River's cock in a move Morgan knew really fucking well. A ghost-touch that made Morgan crazy every single time. "Still feels just as overwhelming after as many times as I've had my bloke up in me, yeah? Brilliant, that."

"Oh, fuck. Honey, shut up," Morgan growled, low and deep. River around him, rocking like that, seeing Simon touching the guy the way he was...it was too fucking much with Simon's words. Too hot, too sharp, too *much*.

Simon sighed, but it wasn't a bad sound. More teasing than anything else. "Right, then. Need something else to do with my mouth." And Simon moved, though Morgan didn't know why. Didn't much care, either, because fuck if River wasn't lifting up just a little, maybe an inch or two, then dropping down again, and "Christ!" Then Simon was back, a brightly coloured wrapper in his hand and Morgan couldn't see the look he gave River, but River was suddenly moving faster, starting to really ride.

Morgan held on tightly to River's hips, tight enough to bruise, but he couldn't help it. Shit, the guy felt good around him. Tighter, somehow, though that didn't seem possible. Then tearing plastic and Simon's hand, rolling pale green over River's bobbing cock, sheathing it as a small burst of something minty wafted to Morgan's nose, and...no. No fucking way. Simon wasn't going to... But he was, Morgan saw. Simon was absolutely going to.

His grip tightened even more on soft skin over muscle and bone, and Morgan held River still, three inches of cock outside River's tight little hole as Simon pushed closer and wrapped his lips around River's shaft. Morgan couldn't see his lover's lips around River, but he knew. Knew because he knew Simon. Knew from the way River was upright so quickly, no longer using Morgan's chest for support or leverage.

"Dude," River groaned. "Dude, that's fucking..." Morgan figured 'awesome' would be the next word, but it didn't make it from River's lips. Instead some strangled, nearly shrill sound filled the fucking air and Morgan smiled a little, then pushed his hips down into the mattress before jabbing them up again, snapping to flush against River's ass just to hear that whimpering, whining whatever one more time.

Time stopped being about seconds or minutes or even hours. Morgan only knew it passed at all by the grunts and moans and short, sharp cries. His body was straining, though. Straining and humping up into River, not rough, exactly, but not smooth, either. Desperate might cover it, but Morgan didn't care if he was.

His arms burned, ached from keeping River right where he was while Simon sucked that long, thin cock sheathed in spearmint flavoured latex, but it wouldn't be much longer. Couldn't be. Not with the way River's hole kept tightening, clamping around Morgan every time he thrust up. Then Simon did something, probably that thing with his tongue that always did it for Morgan, and River was arching even more, hair trailing back, sliding over Morgan's thighs again, slipping between them to tickle his balls, and that was it. The final too much in a world of too much. The too much that pushed Morgan past *almost* and directly into the land of once-fucking-was.

His shout echoed through the room, and try as he might, Morgan couldn't *not* pull River down hard on his throbbing, aching cock, and River cried out right after him, that hole tighter still as Morgan shot long and hard into the latex that had kept him from coming far sooner.

"Oh, man," River gasped a little while later, still sitting on Morgan's cock, though River's shoulders were a little slumped. "Fucking awesome." Then Simon leant up, kissing River lightly before turning to press a matching, slightly deeper kiss to Morgan's lips, sharing the flavour of what passed for mint.

"About to get better, pet," Simon murmured, that weird-ass purring sound in his voice. "Morgan's had his turn, yeah? Bloody well want mine, I do." Fuck, that smirk was sexy, even in profile. "Kept this waiting, just for your lovely ass, mate. What say you just lie on my bloke there and I'll do the rest."

Fuck if Morgan knew when Simon had a chance to get another condom open and on, but he had, and good thing, too. Because River just let out a shaky little laugh and lifted up, pulling himself from around Morgan's softening dick. Then he leant down, legs still spread wide over Morgan's hips, and held himself up, arms to either side of Morgan's shoulders. "This okay, man?" he asked and Morgan couldn't help laughing a little.

"Fine," he answered, feeling lighter inside than he had in ages, probably because River was so open, so honest about loving sex, enjoying it. "Means we can kiss while my honey's fucking you, right?"

River laughed too, even as Simon moved, pushed Morgan's legs apart to make room for Simon's knees. "Fuck yeah, man. Part of the appeal." Then River moaned and pushed down onto him, lips soft and open against Morgan's neck.

Morgan felt Simon's first push into River's body in the way River moved and he moaned, too. His hands found River's sides, stroked golden skin in counterpoint to the way Simon was moving, pulled long blond hair to the side, keeping it out of the way, and when River lifted his head, eyes wide and dreamy, Morgan couldn't resist taking River's mouth in a kiss that started slow and just got deeper, not faster.

One hand in River's hair, the other down on River's hip, somehow, fingers tangling with Simon's as Morgan's lover treated their...their River, Morgan decided...right.

Long, fast thrusts shook River's body, the guy's cock firming up a little between them, and fuck if Morgan's wasn't doing so as well, swampy condom still on or not. Both of them, Morgan realised, because he could feel River's latex between them, too. Fucking Simon, he thought with a grin against River's lips. Always in a hurry.

Of course, sometimes that was a good thing, because Simon was moving faster, harder. He was making that little noise Morgan loved, too. That grunt-growl-whine thing that said Simon was close. So fucking close. He only needed...Morgan dragged his mouth from River's and bit one golden shoulder and River jumped, muscles going tight, and that was it. One more hard, fierce shove from Simon, a shout that rang in Morgan's ears, and then Simon was on them, breathing hard as they toppled, Simon and River slipping to the side, both panting hard.

"Fuck," River said a few minutes later, after condoms were taken care of and a soft, wet cloth came into play. "You dudes really know how to show a guy a good time." And fuck if he didn't sound happy as shit.

Simon laughed, reaching across River's stomach to grip Morgan's hand, and that was...yeah. Perfect. "Party's just getting started, pet," Simon answered, smug and fucking pleased; Morgan could tell. "Hours and hours to go."

Christ. Hours more just might kill him, but Morgan couldn't bring himself to care. Not a single fucking bit.

Chapter Seven

Another Game, this one in Duluth, of all places, and involving the acquisition of information from a very perverted official who had taken great delight in telling River that he swung both ways and wanted to play a bit, but not just with River, but with Moon, too.

It wasn't entirely new, the suggestion, but the fact that the man had wanted to enjoy both of them *at the same time* was more than River could stomach. He loved Moony, yeah. She was his sister, his twin. But he didn't love her like *that*. Not in any way that involved the two of them naked and possibly touching each other. The fucking pervert had for damned sure wanted them to, though. Even offered the twisted and fucking ridiculous opinion that as long as River used a condom, it wouldn't count as incest, or even fucking. Jesus.

Moon hadn't been too happy about it either, though she'd let the fucker live. River wasn't sure he would have done the same, but whatever. It wasn't like the guy was ever likely to tell anyone that he'd been blindsided, knocked out and ripped off by two kids who seemed as sweet and innocent as River and Moon could look when they tried.

He grinned at his sister, offering up a wink for the vicious smile that lingered on her lips, all teeth and fury if anyone knew to look for it. Yeah, underneath that angelic exterior, Moon was what their Dad had called a bitch on wheels. Or was that heels? River never could remember. Either way it fit, though.

"Let it go, Moony," he said softly as they strode down the sidewalk after leaving the cab they'd taken from the disgusting shit's place, the asshole's laptop cradled carefully under River's arm. If the man managed to get himself untied and somehow drag his undoubtedly sore body to a phone, then thought of trying to track down their cab, well. The driver would only be able to say that he'd dropped River and Moon—or Robbie and Mona Simpkins, as their IDs said—at the Fitzgerald Inn, which was exactly where they'd told Councilman Renfrew they were staying when they'd met the slimy man 'accidentally' the day before. The driver would have no way of knowing that they'd ducked inside, then headed out the back and made a beeline for the Sheraton.

With any luck, the rest of the team would have collected the Simpkins' things and done automated check-out when River had called them on his secure cell two hours earlier.

They went in separately, just in case the sick creep had thought of calling other hotels in the area. Less likely to stand out if they weren't together, so River headed straight to the front desk across the near-cavernous lobby, only three buttons fastened on his shirt and ready to make sure that, even if someone asked, the front desk wouldn't say a word about him.

He bypassed the leather couches and chairs that looked so damned comfortable while Moon waited outside. She would follow in a minute or two with the stolen computer and make her way to the elevators while River acted as a distraction.

Shit, his feet hurt from the too-tight, too-expensive shoes 'Robbie Simpkins' favoured. River was more the bare feet type when possible, though he didn't hate his worn Birks. Which were back in his rooms at HQ, damn it.

"Hey, man," River droned out, catching the clerk's attention. "Is there a house phone I can use? I have a…um, an appointment. You know." No innocent grin now. Not at all. River was smirking like the high-priced rent-boy he was pretending to be. Lewd. Lascivious. Jaded and worn. "I just need to call up, make sure my clie…friend is ready for me. Hey, maybe I'll just hit the bar for a while. I'm sorta early."

Yeah, that had desk-dude suspicious, all right. "You're kinda cute," River added, giving the guy as much of a look as he could with the counter between them. "Tell you what. If you take a break, I'll blow you for a hundred bucks. You'll be screaming inside five minutes."

Shit. Just shit. The dude actually looked like he was thinking about it. His pimply brow was furrowed and everything. Fuck, River could almost *see* the guy trying to do the math in his head. Then "I'm not gay. But maybe next time," the guy muttered, and thank fucking God. "The bar's over there. Do me a favour and walk slow. I really like your hair."

River tossed the man another of his rent-boy smiles, and rolled his eyes when he turned away. Moon would be on her way up to the eighth floor by then, he knew. Eighth floor and the room Simon had chosen to be their coordination centre for the Game. Ten minutes in the bar and River could follow. Then…oh, then they could all get the fuck out of Minnesota. They'd go back to HQ and River could wash the slime of their target's suggestions from his skin and hopefully from his mind, too. Fuck, he might never get it up again, just from the idea of it all still rattling around in his brain, making him want to puke.

Hours later, River moaned around Morgan's covered cock, his own sheathed in latex and Simon's mouth. The fingers pushing in and out of him, spreading his hole, were Simon's, and it didn't matter how often they'd done exactly that before, it was fucking awesome each and every time.

Eventually, Simon would pull back, slip out from under River's body. Simon would kneel behind him, push inside, fuck him until River wanted to scream. He wouldn't though. Wouldn't scream. He'd just stay right there on all fours, head bobbing up and down on Morgan's cock. Right up until Simon throbbed, grunted, arched hard into him and filled latex with hot cum. Then Morgan would pull away from River's mouth and take Simon's place. He would open River even more with that huge fucking cock that couldn't miss a guy's prostate if Morgan tried.

And Simon would kiss him, River knew. Would drive his tongue deep into River's mouth, swallowing moans and cries easily, feeding them back in a circle of pleasure River had never known existed. Then they'd collapse together and River would barely be able to do more than moan "dude" until long after Simon and Morgan had left for their own room.

Yeah, River thought, pushing his head lower, taking just a bit more hot, thick, cherry-condom-flavoured cock into his throat, it was shaping up to be a damned good night.

* * * *

Australia. Fucking brilliant. Nice weather, granted, and for the most part, not a soul Simon had run into in Sydney had done anything but offer up smiles and good days and whatever the fuck else. Odd, that, though perhaps he'd been living in America too long. He recalled a certain amount of fare-thee-well-fellow from his youth in England, after all. Still it was bloody fucking annoying, all that good cheer.

"Probably be different outside the tourist and business districts, I'll wager," he grumbled to himself, though he was mostly listening to what little he was getting from the transmitter in River's clothing. Bloke was doing a right good job, if the mark's moaning and groaning were any sort of sign.

"What are they up to now?" Morgan asked, dropping a kiss on Simon's head that made him smile.

"More of the same," Simon answered, trying not to snap the words out no matter how much he wanted to. Bloody hell, three Games since he and Morgan had taken up with River, and this was the first time he had needed to get down and dirty with a target. It shouldn't have bothered him. Simon knew that, kept telling himself as much. Shouldn't have. Did.

"Christ, is he going for a record?" Yeah, Morgan didn't sound any happier about it than Simon was, which was something of a comfort. "It's been...what? Close to a fucking hour? Shit."

Simon snorted. "Count yourself lucky that you don't have to bloody well listen to it. 'Oh, Ricky. That's so good. You're so big, Ricky, filling up my little Asian

cunny. Oh, do that again.' Bloody shrill, the twat."
Okay, maybe he wasn't hiding his irritation as well as
he'd like.

And maybe, Simon told himself, he was pissed off
that River was lasting so bloody long with the
corporate slag, no matter that he was keeping her
busy in the hotel room above Simon and Morgan
while Moon put her breaking and entering skills to
use at the cow's penthouse apartment.

Moon was more than good at her job, though. Small
consolation as it was, at least Simon was sure of that
much. If the forty-five-year-old bitch screaming for
River really was selling her corporation out to the
Chinese, Moon would find the proof and they could
get the fuck out of Sydney. They were well ahead of
schedule, the slut giving it up as soon as River had
batted his pretty blue eyes at her. Unexpected, but
welcome, that.

Morgan was growling beside him, the sound soft
enough, deep enough in his bloke's chest that Simon
thought Morgan likely wasn't aware of doing it at all.
But yeah, that sound was just what Simon was feeling,
as well. Un-bloody-professional, but there it was. He
resented the fuck out of River doing his job like that
and so did Morgan. It was ridiculous. Insane. Stupid
as a box of rocks that they were bothered by it.

The comm on the bed buzzed quietly but Simon
ignored it. Morgan would answer and leave Simon to
listen to more pleas of *faster* and *harder* and *God, yes,
just like that*. And Morgan did, his voice calm and cool,
so normal that Simon figured he was the only one
who could hear the strange mix of anger and
disappointment there, because he felt those things
himself.

"Good," Morgan said, and "okay, I'm checking right now." Then the sound of clicking and, when Simon glanced behind him, Morgan was on the computer set up on the desk in their room. "Yeah, I got it, Moon. Hold on, let me make sure." A few more clicks and Morgan laughed. Just once, but it was enough. Their work was done. They had the information they needed. They could leave, assuming River ever finished his bloody slutting about.

"She's headed back, Si," Morgan said quietly a few seconds later. "Oh, and she says that whore's security is for shit. I just forwarded the files to HQ, so as soon as we get confirmation we can reformat a few times and get the fuck out of here, honey."

"Yeah? Somebody should tell bloody fucking River that. Bloke sounds like he could keep going all night and then some." Sod it all, he was snarling. At Morgan. Shit. But Morgan's hands were on Simon's shoulders, thumbs digging in, and Simon knew Morgan understood.

A long, soft sigh from behind him, then Morgan's voice again, this time sounding curious, confused, maybe even a little bit hopeless, like Morgan really didn't have a single clue. "What do we do, Si? How can we…"

There were so many endings to that sentence, but all of them boiled down to one single thing. How could they keep doing what they were? *Could* they? River had been incredibly up front about still doing his job. Hadn't had even a single moment of doubt when they'd first started whatever the blue bloody fuck they were doing, the three of them. Wasn't the bloke's fault that Simon—and Morgan, obviously—had gone and become unexpectedly attached. Attached enough to be jealous, of all things. Wasn't anything they'd planned on.

"I don't have any idea, love," Simon admitted sourly, though he let Morgan's hands, fingers, thumbs relax him a bit. He was too tense, anyway. Tight, like a fucking bow strung to its limit. "Figure we can either suck it up or end it all, yeah?" He sighed and nodded when Morgan's hands stilled for a second before starting their massage again. "Don't want to any more than you do, love, but...not sure how long I can stand listening to our bloke putting it to whoever the fuck needs convincing or distracting or whatever the hell they need. Can't ask him to stop, he's too bloody good at getting in and getting it done. So to speak."

Another sigh, and Simon knew that if he looked he'd see Morgan trying to put on that stoic face that fooled everyone but Simon. "We'll work it out, then," Morgan finally said, and bloody fucking hell, Simon hoped so. He truly did. Their current situation was nigh-on intolerable.

The first thing Simon did when River finally turned up over half an hour later was strip River off and hustle the bloke into the shower, his own clothes left carelessly on the floor in a trail. Hands and soap, sliding all over that soft skin, paying careful attention to every part, but especially those that had been inside the bitch Simon hated right then. The bitch who'd left bloody fucking claw marks on River's back for all the world to see. Like she was staking some sort of sodding claim.

Morgan joined them about ten minutes in, after Moon had returned safely and headed off to join the rest of the team two floors down, and that was better, somehow. More hands to clean their boy, to wash the overbearing scent of what was likely a very expensive and overly fragrant perfume from River's skin.

Get their bloke free of the twat's stench, and maybe they could pretend it had never happened. River seemed to get it, too, because he wasn't struggling, wasn't even asking what the fuck Simon was doing, or Morgan either. Instead, he just stood there under the hot water, eyes closed. He did let out one soft, grunted moan when Morgan started lathering that long, tangled hair, though.

Soap, shampoo, conditioner. River's toothbrush, loaded down with paste. Minutes that seemed like hours before River spat and rinsed. Lifted his face to the spray and let it pour into his mouth, the force pushing the last minty froth out. And finally, finally, River relaxed. Relaxed and leaned against them, against Simon and Morgan, just a tiny shiver announcing that River hadn't particularly enjoyed what he'd been doing with the Asian dragon-lady, which shouldn't have made Simon feel better, but bloody fucking hell, it did. It really and truly did.

Morgan too, obviously, because a small smile flashed at the corners of Morgan's lips. Just enough for Simon to see before it vanished as quickly as it had arrived. "You okay, Riv?" Morgan said then, raising one big hand to River's face, palming cheek and jaw and neck, sliding his fingertips into River's hair, Morgan's thumb brushing lightly just below one cheekbone. And River shuddered.

"Fuck, man," River answered, and Simon had never heard him sound like that before; especially not after sex. Not a laugh or a chuckle or even a single tone that implied River had enjoyed himself. "That was one freaky chick. I…man. Thank fuck I finally came. I was barely even keeping it up."

It was the perfect time for one of the snarky remarks Simon so enjoyed coming up with, and yet he didn't want to. Didn't feel even the slightest urge to make light of it, even though a large part of him, carefully hidden behind what Simon hoped was a serious expression, was dancing. Celebrating at hearing what had taken so long.

"Sorry, baby," Morgan murmured to River, thumb still moving on the bloke's face and Simon blinked. Bloody hell. Baby? Well, yeah. And River wasn't making a single sound to object, so that was good. Baby, it was. Just as Simon called River pet, more often than not. Whilst naked, in any case. "What can we do, Riv?" Morgan went on, still soft, low, soothing, sort of. "Washed her off you already. What do you need now? Whatever it is, baby, it's yours."

True, Simon decided. "Name it, pet, and we'll bloody well make it happen." And maybe he could handle it all after all, Simon thought. If this was the way of it, if he and Morgan could make River theirs again after any more Games, then…yeah, he could do that. Morgan could too. Simon would have to remember to talk it over later. Much later.

"I just…I need you," River whispered, the words almost lost under the sound of the water and Simon's beating heart. "Both of you guys, okay? I fucking need you, dudes."

"Here or bed, baby," Morgan spoke before Simon could, but that was fine. Brilliant, even, because the slightly lost tone to River's voice had a fully unexpected lump forming in Simon's throat.

River leaned harder against them both, like he didn't want even an inch between them, and neither did Simon. He wanted them close as close could be. Wanted River and Morgan around him, touching him.

Then a shiver raced through River's body and Simon swallowed hard. "Here," Simon answered, though the question hadn't been aimed at him. "Here, love, where our bloke can be nice and warm, yeah?" Even with being almost entirely sure it wasn't a physical chill River was experiencing, the warmth of water and skin couldn't hurt.

River just nodded and Morgan pulled away. "Okay. Okay, I'll be right back. Rubbers," Morgan explained to Simon's arched brow, and yeah. Yeah, condoms. Simon had almost forgotten.

"Be right here, love, me and our bloke."

He held River close, pressing a slow kiss to lips that tasted of mint and River, with nothing of the horrid bitch left, thank bloody Christ. And when River's mouth opened to him almost desperately, Simon dove inside, tongue lashing back and forth, tracing teeth, gums, the ridges on the roof of River's mouth. Then Morgan was back, packets and lube in hand, and they possibly stretched River too quickly and not enough, but he was just as anxious as Simon was, just as needy...and when Morgan pushed in, River didn't cry out or gasp or even talk.

He just bit his lip and pressed back, eyes closed tightly, hiding that blue-blue gaze from Simon, River's body still shaking, still shuddering. Then Morgan's hand was around River's long, thin dick and Simon smiled a bit, took the lube from the edge of the tub and moments later drove two slick fingers into his own anus.

Morgan saw him; of course he did. Those brown eyes widened, surprised but heated, like Morgan wanted to see, like he'd hoped but not dared to believe. They'd never had River inside, after all. Neither of them. It hadn't happened for whatever reason, but it was about to. Simon was firmly committed to the idea.

Digits, moving in and out. More lube, more slip and slide, slick and warming fast. Then the other condom, opened and rolled over River's prick, and yeah, River felt that. Thought he'd be getting sucked off, Simon figured. But instead of dropping to his knees, Simon turned.

With his hands braced against the shower wall, ceramic hard and glossy, wet with condensation and steam, Simon leant, bent, spread his legs as much as he could, then gave Morgan a nod over his shoulder. He didn't think River even noticed Morgan moving him forward, the tiny steps going in time with Morgan's slow, shallow thrusts. But River definitely knew it when Morgan's hand had the tip of that pretty, sheathed cock right up against Simon's hole.

"What..." River started, but Morgan thrust hard, pushed River in, and Simon pressed back, opening for that bulb of flesh, and River let loose something that combined sigh and moan and yelp as they moved him until his balls slapped against Simon's, River's cock heavy and deep and feeling far thicker than it looked.

"Si?" he heard and Simon nodded, swallowed, met Morgan's eyes then River's, because they were open now. As open as Simon's body.

Simon nodded again, for River. "Yeah. Bloody fucking yeah. Just like this."

Still mostly silent, they moved together, Simon moaning softly, Morgan humming so quiet and low it was barely audible. And River...oh, River was right up against Simon's back, arms wrapped around Simon like he was the only real thing in an imaginary world. Then Morgan's arms were there as well, hands over River's while they shifted, strained, heaved together and apart by inches, sweat rinsing away as the shower continued to pour clean, wet heat over them all.

River was still shaking when he came. Simon could feel it even through his own orgasm. But it felt different. Better. And Morgan was still moving behind them, slow and steady, pushing River's spent cock in and in until finally Simon felt even that motion cease, giving way to a moment of stillness broken only by one soft, drawn-out grunt leaving Morgan's lips.

They were ahead of schedule, Simon reminded himself as they lay in the hotel's king sized bed a little while later. Substantially ahead, really. Three days or so. They could afford a nap and some time to soothe River a bit more.

He smiled at Morgan over the bloke between them, and squeezed the two hands that were holding one of his own, River's stomach right there under their fingertips. Morgan smiled back with an ease Simon hadn't really expected, but he was happy with it, all the same.

Bloody hell, it had been a long sodding day. Ended well, though, Simon thought as he listened to River's breathing slow, become steady and deep; then Morgan's followed along. Yeah, Simon told himself as he pulled the sheet and blanket up a bit higher and pressed closer to River's side. Ended well, indeed.

Chapter Eight

They could have done worse, Morgan knew. Could have done much worse than to get all...wrapped up in River. At least the guy always came back to them. Let them hold on. But fuck if he didn't want more, and Morgan knew Simon did, too. They'd sort of talked about it, or as much as they ever did. Hell, he and Simon seemed to have some sort of shorthand or something between them, or at least were on the same page often enough that too many words weren't needed.

Good thing, too, because Morgan had never been a talk-it-to-death guy and he wasn't planning on turning into one. Ever. Simon got him, deep down, and Morgan was pretty fucking sure River knew exactly what the deal was, too. Hell, they would have just moved River right the fuck in if it wasn't for Jericho.

Yeah, his half-daughter — or whatever the right term was because they for damned sure hadn't figured one out yet — was cool with Morgan and Simon being together. Rico was cool with Simon sharing their rooms, too. Rico probably knew exactly what he and Simon were to each other, likely owing to her odd skills, though Morgan generally made a point of not fucking thinking about it. The girl was twelve, though. Old enough to understand about people being gay, and Morgan hadn't bothered to pretend he and Simon were just good friends or whatever shit other guys might try with their...wards.

Yeah, ward worked. He and Rico shared a certain amount of DNA, and he'd raised her pretty much from a baby, so guardian and sort-of father. Fucking smart kid, but she got that from her mother. Shit, they both missed Ellie, even after more than two years. Probably always would. It was so difficult for Rico to accept that her mom was gone and wouldn't be coming back; to know that Ellie had died to keep her safe. But on the whole, Rico was doing well and that was all Ellie had ever wanted, so they dealt, the two of them.

The three of them, really, because Simon was just as much a part of Rico's life as Morgan, since the FGC had taken Morgan and Rico in. So it wasn't the gay thing that had him freaked. It was the Morgan and Simon *and River* thing that Morgan was worried about. Even with being as ahead of the fucking curve as Rico was, she was still a kid. How the fuck could he explain that he and Simon were fine but they had a boyfriend? A *shared* boyfriend. And forget the part where River still fucked around during Games, because nobody else would ever understand that, much less a twelve-year-old girl.

So, yeah. No moving River in. It wasn't fucking possible, no matter how much he and Simon might want it. Rico's peace of mind mattered more than pretty much anything.

Morgan frowned, glared at the screen beside him and hit the reset button before reloading his weapon with a fresh clip. Shit, he was off. Not by a lot, but even a tiny fucking bit could be enough to get him or one of his team injured or dead. They might not do high-risk Games, but there had been more than one firefight in the past and likely would be again. He needed to be sharp, damn it. Needed to pay attention, or at least hone his skills enough that he was flawless even while his head was full of shit that wasn't relevant to the field.

Another clip fired, another less than satisfactory read-out. Fuck. Ninety-six per cent on his targets. Only ninety-fucking-six. Shit.

New clip, new round of firing. The Club blew through more ammunition in a week than all the police departments in a hundred mile radius did in a year, Morgan was sure. Then again, it made sense. Gentlemen didn't have uniforms that inspired people to run. And the people the Club went up against weren't the running kind anyway.

"Okay," Morgan muttered to himself as the screen flashed again. "Ninety-seven. Better, but not good enough." Ninety-nine would be satisfactory. Good enough that he'd feel relatively secure in his ability to keep Simon and River safe in the field. The rest of their team too, but Morgan had his fucking priorities, and they were primarily wrapped around one dark haired, greyish-blue eyed Brit and one twenty-four-year-old kid with long blond hair and the bluest fucking eyes Morgan had ever seen. It might not be Club policy, but fuck if Morgan wouldn't look after his own first.

Just like he'd been more than willing to kill or even die to keep Rico safe while they'd been running from fucking NovoTech, he'd do the same for his lovers. Simon would look after Rico if it came to that, if Morgan didn't come back from a Game someday. If neither of them returned, Patrice would take over. Ballsy bitch that she was, Morgan knew she loved Rico, maybe close to as much as he loved her himself.

"Yeah, that's not fucking fatalistic, is it Morgan?" he snarled softly. "Fuck. Focus, man."

He did his damnedest on the next round, eyes darting to follow the flashing targets that flitted quickly around the range. Squeeze and release, squeeze and release. *Blam-blam-blam.* One shot after another, hands steady, mind skipping back and forth between shooting and trying to find a way to resolve the different areas of his life.

Squeeze and release. Adjust for recoil, though that part was automatic, muscle memory. Never hurt to pay attention.

Rico, who'd been the most important thing in his life since the day she was born.

Squeeze and release. Frown at the missed target.

Simon, who made things better just by being there, by caring.

Squeeze and release. Smile a little because yeah, that was one dead target. Good.

River, who was supposed to be something casual but had turned into so much more than Morgan or Simon had ever expected. Desert-raised, home-schooled, surfer-boy-sounding River. Slut but not. Somehow theirs.

Squeeze and release, *blam-blam-blam.* Three shots, targets found, one only wounded because it went from green to yellow, rather than red. Shit.

"Not your best performance ever," Morgan heard and he lowered his gun, hit the end-session button on the small console beside him, and sighed.

"I know, Patrice. I'm a little distracted, okay?" Simon would have had some smug, snarky insult to throw at the woman, but Morgan didn't have that kind of relationship with her. That antagonistic but somehow friendly respect was beyond Morgan's capacity.

"No," she answered as Morgan turned to face her, nine mil tucked into the back of his pants for the moment. Yeah, she looked...something. Disappointed maybe, or possibly concerned. He couldn't be sure. "Actually, the last thing it is, is 'okay'. I don't think I've seen you shoot that poorly since a week after you started practising here, Morgan."

Yeah, he already knew that. "Duh. That's why I've been on the range for an hour. I'm just..." Morgan frowned and shook his head. "I don't know. Off. Just...off the mark. I'll get it figured out."

A considering look flashed in Patrice's pale green eyes and fuck if Morgan didn't want to hide. Fuck if he wasn't ashamed that his personal issues were messing with his work. He might not be in the field right then, but it was still his job to stay sharp. Ready. To always be prepared. Like a fucking boy scout. With guns and the willingness to kill whenever necessary.

"I'm sure you will," Patrice said after a moment, and Morgan relaxed a little. Patrice never blew smoke. If she said she was sure, then she was sure, and that was one hell of a relief. "Fortunately, you have a month to work out whatever it is that's bothering you. The Belize Game has been cancelled. The client was unable to meet our price with anything but promises." She gave him an arch look and crossed her arms under her breasts. "I suggest that you use the time wisely. You do appear to need it."

Fuck if he didn't want to hit the bitch. But wanting and doing were two different things and Morgan wouldn't hit a woman who wasn't trying to kill him any more than he'd hit a child. "Yeah, no shit, Lady," he grunted, feeling grumpy and, yeah, off balance.

A blink. Just one, but enough for Morgan to know he'd surprised her somehow. "I'm going to schedule you for a session with Doctor Alterowitz," she said then and Morgan frowned again. He didn't need a fucking shrink; he just needed to figure out...well, maybe. Maybe she had a point. "I'll have his assistant email you with time and date. I can't afford to have even one member of one of our best teams going through a crisis that's affecting his performance. This is not optional, Morgan."

"Got it," Morgan answered, stepping around her and heading for the door to the outer chamber. He stopped, looking down at her hand, so suddenly on his arm. "I'm not fucking around, Patrice," he added. "I'll go. Your judgement is probably better than mine right now."

Well, fuck him. He'd actually surprised a laugh out of her. A small one, but still pretty cool. Then she squeezed his arm lightly and pulled her hand away, though she followed him from the firing range.

"You're much more reasonable than that man of yours," she said in the outer chamber. "Meaning Simon, of course. The Stone boy, on the other hand, tends to roll with the punches. Or he did. He's been a bit distracted of late, as well. Hopefully the next month or so will get him back on track, too."

Then she was gone, out into the main corridor, leaving Morgan to gape like a landed fish.

"Patrice knows about River," Morgan whispered to Simon an hour or so later, after sparring with Tink and getting knocked on his ass repeatedly. He'd done pretty well anyway, though. "I mean she knows about *us* and River." Fuck. Simon was going to...Morgan blinked. Okay, Simon was going to snort. Not really the reaction Morgan had expected. At all.

"Well, of course bitchy-bitch knows, love," Simon murmured back, leaning both elbows on the cafeteria table. "Run the team under her direct control, don't I? Hardly surprising that she'd check the bloody reels on all of us from time to time."

Christ. That explained it. He'd actually grown so used to the idea that they were all constantly under surveillance that Morgan didn't even think about it anymore. Wasn't even embarrassed that there were people listening in all day and night, no matter where in HQ he was. He was definitely embarrassed that he'd sort of forgotten, though. And wait.

"She said River's been 'distracted' lately, too," Morgan remembered, said, announced. "Oh, and the Belize gig is off."

One dark brow arched and Simon nodded, just enough for Morgan to know they would talk about it later. Back in their rooms where the other Gentlemen and Ladies in the cafeteria wouldn't overhear. "Right, then. So. How's your day been, aside from that? And eat your bloody lunch. Your body needs the energy to heal those pretty bruises Tink left. Only see the one on your cheek, granted, but I know the chit well enough to be sure there's a colourful assortment under your togs, don't I?"

Yeah, Morgan told himself as he dug in to the salad and lasagne on his tray, Simon was definitely right about that. Of course, Simon would kiss every one later, as Morgan knew from experience. It actually made the small pains worthwhile.

* * * *

Oh, man. A whole extra month before he and Moon had to head out on another Game. Too cool. Except he shouldn't be thinking it was cool and River knew it. He should be raring to go, to get back out in the field, to move on to the next mission. But man, he just wasn't. Even with being able to hang out at the Ranch whenever he wasn't training to keep himself in fighting form, he should be anxious to get back to it. He shouldn't be sitting by the pond in the third pasture, watching the horses drink.

Maybe he was coming down with something, River thought, but he felt fine. Nothing going on with his lungs or shit like that. Nothing felt...wrong. "Aside from the Games," he said to the colt across the pond, but the animal just flicked an ear and went on drinking. Was it still called a colt when it was close to a year? River wasn't sure. Didn't much care, either. He had bigger problems. Like loving his job but hating what he had to do sometimes.

It was crazy. He loved sex. Always had, from the first time he'd got his dick wet with Sally Thompson and her boyfriend Raul. Not both at the same time, but yeah. Hell, sex was one of the things he'd always been good at.

He still was, for fuck's sake. Still loved it, too. But not on the fucking Games, damn it. "I'm sick. I must be. Man." Because there was no other explanation. He loved sex; loved fucking. When it was with Morgan and Simon. But for some weird-ass reason, even thinking about the random sex he'd had before and would probably have to have again left him..."Not cold," River told the drinking animal, "sick. Leaves me feeling fucking queasy, as Mom would say." He sighed long and hard. "Shit. I'm so fucked up."

"You're heart-sick." The words came from behind him and River jumped, even as he turned and tried to find some sort of defensive position that would let him become something other than dead. Or thoroughly shamed, since only FGC folk would even be on the Ranch. "Hi, River." Jericho grinned and River mustered up the best smile he could.

"Keeta. Hey, what's up?" The girl grinned like she always did, red hair tied back, green eyes bright. Man, just what he needed. A reminder of exactly why he was avoiding down below.

He knew Jericho pretty well. Hell, he worked with Morgan and Simon and they were more or less the girl's dads, so River had seen her, spent time with her, loads of times. Sure, she was a little strange, but what the fuck, so was River. She liked him, though River wasn't sure she would if she ever found about what he was doing with her parents or whatever.

"Nothing," Jericho answered, still grinning as she looked out at the pond. "The fish are getting lazy. Zeke keeps throwing them food so they're starting to get used to it." A tiny frown. "Another generation or two and they won't remember how to feed themselves any other way."

Yeah, that was Keeta. Always thinking about things most kids her age wouldn't even consider. It was really pretty cool. Hell, she'd even understood the whole Keeta thing right off. He'd called her chiquita one day and she'd told him, very seriously, that she wasn't a little girl. Chica had earned a frown for being too generic. Her words, not his. Keeta, though—or

Quita, really—made her smile. So Keeta she was, just between the two of them. And he'd come to like it even more since he'd started sleeping with Morgan and Simon. Morgan called Jericho Rico, after all, and Simon...well, Simon seemed to flip-flop between Princess and Petal. Calling Jericho Keeta sort of let River feel like he was a bigger part of things than he was. Than he was ever likely to be, he reminded himself.

He didn't have any right to want more, though. He'd known what it was before he, Morgan and Simon had even started up. Sex. Fun. Fucking. Nothing else. Which didn't stop him from *wanting* more, and maybe feeling a little bit resentful that he couldn't have it.

"That's 'progress', right?" River drawled the words out, pushing his thoughts away to focus on the conversation. Jericho might be twelve, but she was damned smart. For damned sure smart enough to know when someone was paying attention. "Like...people used to know how to hunt. Stick your average dude in the wilderness without a credit card or grocery store in sight *now*, the guy would probably starve to death."

Jericho nodded and sat down next to him, all long, skinny arms and legs. Kid looked like some sort of militant elf or pixie or something in her camouflage shorts and matching T-shirt. "Even if you gave him a gun," she said, clearly agreeing, and yeah. She was more like an adult in a kid suit. "Then there's people like us. We can't function in the real world any better than they could in ours. Not for long, anyway. Like...can you imagine how it would feel to be *out there*"—Jericho gestured broadly—"and know that was it? That you could never come back to the Club or the Ranch; never be who you really are?"

River frowned deeply and shook his head. "I grew up out there. I could stay. I'd be fine. So would you."

The girl snorted and she sounded so much like Simon that River almost laughed. Softer, daintier, but yeah, like Simon. "I've read your file, River. You and Moony, you might not have grown up right here, but your dad raised you Club. Just like I grew up running and hiding and shooting people with Morgan because they wanted to take me away and do bad things to me, you grew up learning a lot of the same stuff the Gentlemen and Ladies learn, but way earlier. So we're not normal. We'll never *be* normal. Just like my sibs Morgan and Simon took out of Madam's hole of horrors."

Whoa. There were so many things wrong with what Jericho had said that River couldn't even count them. Not wrong like she was lying, but wrong that she even knew that much. Mostly, though, "You read my file? How the fu…who showed you my file?" Jesus. River hadn't even seen his file and it was *his*.

Another smile, toothy and strangely winning, took up residence on Jericho's face. She pulled a handful of grass out by the roots and tossed the blades one by one into the water. "I hacked the system. Duh." That grin got a little bit wider, though River would have bet it wasn't possible. "Uncle Director's got the coolest system ever! And he's got even more on you Stones than Patty does."

Shit. Jericho had hacked the Director's computer. And called him Uncle. And seemed to be implying — flat out stating — that she knew more about River and Moon than Patrice, the Events Coordinator. Fuck.

"Why?" Yeah, that was the question. "Why were you even curious, Keeta? I mean, for real. I woulda told you whatever you wanted to know." Mostly. Except about what he actually did during Games. Which was undoubtedly in the Director's files, and...fuck. Just fuck. Man.

A tiny shrug, almost not even there, but River saw it; then more blades of grass, pulled and sorted and tossed one at a time. "Um. 'Cause I like you and you made Morgan and Simon happy right at first but now they're kind of freaked because they don't like your Games any more but they know it's your job so they're trying to be strong. Duh. So I wanted to find out everything about you and I did."

She gave him a look then, unlike any River had ever seen from her before, and it was...fuck, almost scary. Like she was looking right into him instead of just *at* him. Jesus. Whoa.

"Then I figured I should talk to you," Jericho went on, still sounding like a kid, but also just *not*. "You're really, really loud, River, and you think you know what you want but you don't know why yet. When you do, you need to say so, otherwise..." Another shrug, bigger and much more visible. "Whatever. Hey, do you think Marcus and Tanner would let me have a horse like that?" She pointed at the colt that had finished drinking and was walking away.

Shit, she changed like the wind, River decided. One minute sounding all...fuck. She knew. Knew what River was doing with Morgan and Simon. And she didn't sound upset or freaked out, and... What the fuck did she mean about them, anyway? They were freaked? And he'd *made* — past tense — his lovers happy, which sort of meant he didn't any more, and...

Okay, welcome back to the spinning head full of distractions, for fuck's sake.

"Do you?"

River blinked and tried to remember. Oh, right. Horse. Yeah. He shrugged, imitating her motion. "I don't know. Maybe." He frowned. "You'd probably have to take care of it, though, and I don't know what your schedule's like."

Jericho laughed, the sound tinkling like the pixie she resembled. "The other kids will help if I ask them to. Well, maybe not Seven and Thirteen. They're still scared of Dog. But Three and Ten will. Seventeen's too little, I think. She's only four, but she could watch."

What the...? "Numbers?" Weird. Weird enough to have him back in the moment, anyway.

That grin again, though River thought it was maybe a little bit sad, somehow. "Madam raised them in the lab. They didn't ever have names and now they don't know how to answer to anything but their numbers." Jericho's nose wrinkled. "That bitch called me Specimen One when she got me. I'm glad Morgan killed her."

Okay. Kind of supported the girl's whole theory that Club people weren't normal. Even so, "Morgan lets you talk like that?" Just a question, really. Curiosity. Man, Morgan cussed like a sailor, himself.

Jericho giggled quietly. "Morgan doesn't really like it but it's his own fault for not stopping me when I was little. He only gets upset when I say 'fuck'. I'm not supposed to say that till I'm eighteen."

"Got it, Keeta. I won't tell." River winked and Jericho giggled again before falling silent and just sitting there with him, watching the water move as fish swam, horses drank and blades of grass drifted slowly, making tiny ripples on the surface. It was a simple silence. Easy. Strange to be experiencing it with a kid, but whatever. River didn't really notice the passage of time in the peace and quiet, and when the sound of a bell from the dining hall sounded in the distance, he blinked, surprised.

"I should probably get back if I want to eat up here," he said, giving Jericho a smile born of not worrying for the last little while. It was strange to feel so easy, so at rest, because he thought he really should be worried, especially with what the girl had said about Morgan and Simon, but River figured he'd get all weirded out later. For the moment, he was cool with just being. Breathing in and out.

Jericho shrugged but got up when he did, then she grinned and slipped her hand into his. "My Mom died," she said from out of nowhere, as far as River could tell. "I didn't want her to, but she did."

River nodded slowly as they started across the pasture, his eyes on the ground watching for the inevitable proof of horses. "Yeah, same with my Dad."

"Sometimes people leave because they don't have a choice," Jericho went on, and that tone was in her voice again, the one that said she was more than just a kid, no matter how advanced. "And sometimes people leave because they can."

River nodded again, but he didn't speak. What could he say? Man, the girl was just stating the facts, and he knew it. His own mother had taken off just as soon as he and Moon turned eighteen. Things to do, she'd said.

Then Jericho stopped, her grip on River's hand halting him, too. Her eyes were solemn but there was still a little smile on her lips, which was just strange, but whatever. She was a strange kid in general. Of course, River had already known that.

"But you know what?" she asked then, and River just looked at her. "Sometimes people only leave so they can come back, River. And you don't know it was right for them to go until you see how they come back. Hey, do you think Cook made meatloaf tonight? I always get extra sauce when I'm up here and Cook made meatloaf."

Regular kid again, just like that. Jesus. Her changes were about to make him dizzy. "I guess we're about to find out, Keeta," River answered with a grin. "Come on."

Jericho grinned her shining grin again and nearly skipped beside him. "Hey, River?" she said as they entered the main yard, "I don't care what you do in the field. Just what you do with Morgan and Simon. You're all way more fun when you're happy." Another giggle and Jericho let go of his hand to skip into the mess hall, leaving River staring after her for a moment before he sat down, right there on the small wooden porch by the door. Then he laughed and laughed and laughed, sure he'd gone completely crazy and just as sure that he hadn't.

Keeta had a point, though. Stop worrying about shit he couldn't do anything about and focus on making the things he *could* affect as good as possible. Yeah.

"Dude," he muttered to himself as he wiped the tears of too much hard laughter from his face. "That is one freaky little chick. Cool, but freaky." Then he picked himself up and headed inside where he got meatloaf—because apparently Cook had been expecting Jericho—and joined her, and Zeke, their friend who worked security up on the Ranch, for dinner.

Chapter Nine

The only thing that made River's mouth feel worlds-away better than it had on the numerous other occasions that Simon had felt it around his aching prick was the fact that there was no latex involved. Well, that and that it had been River's idea. No muss, no fuss, just a grin and River's hand dropping the packet on the floor right before giving Simon a wink and then...yeah, those perfect lips, tight around him. Bloody fucking hot, in more ways than one.

Morgan obviously agreed, because the bloke was just a couple of feet away on River's bed. Naked, scooted up high enough to lean against the wall, eyes locked on Simon and River while Morgan slid his big hand up and down the amazing cock that made Simon scream on a near daily basis.

"Fuck, love," Simon said, grinning at the sheer heat in his own voice. "Our bloke's got a mouth on him like a Hoover, yeah?" His hips rocked, feeding just a bit more hard, bare flesh into River's wet mouth, over that flexing tongue. He'd already known River gave good head, but this? Without the bloody rubber? Well, as River was so fond of saying, it was fucking awesome.

Morgan grunted, his hand keeping up slow, easy strokes to his own dick as he watched, but Simon saw the heat in Morgan's eyes. Saw the wanton desire. "Christ, Si. You should see your face. Like you just found fucking Heaven, honey."

Well, maybe he had, Simon decided. River's lips around him, Simon gripping hanks of long blond hair, hips stuttering in and out of that pretty sodding mouth...and the suction that threatened to have Simon getting his end away in record bloody time. "Think I might have done, at that." Groaned more than stated, but that was fine. Yeah, just fucking fine.

River was anything but a passive participant, too, what with the way he moved his hands over Simon's thighs. Up the front, around the sides, little grab at Simon's ass, then down the backs of Simon's legs to his knees before starting up the cycle again. All the while taking him in, mouth moving closer and closer to the base of Simon's cock, tongue flicking fast circles around the tip of Simon's shaft every time River pulled back. Fucking hell. Heaven. Whichever.

Those blue-blue eyes were looking up at him when Simon dragged his gaze from Morgan, shining-hot-blue. A little bit wild, a lot wanton, and Simon barely stifled a disappointed groan when River's mouth pulled back and left him. "I'm just getting started, man," River said with a grin. Then the bloke shot a look to the bed and smiled even more. "Morgan. Dude. Save it, man. You're next."

Lips on Simon's sac, that wet tongue sliding over his balls, and fuck. Just bloody fuck. "Yeah...like that, pet. Just like...yeah." River's mouth on his bollocks, his hands stopping their cycle when one went for Simon's dick, fingers tight and just right around him. River's other hand squeezing Simon's ass in time with those firm licks and small sucks to thin, tender skin over delicate bits. Too good. River was skilled even with latex. Without was a bloody fucking brass band doing its thing to a right appreciative audience, and... "Pet!"

Too fast, but they had hours yet, which only meant Simon didn't need to try holding back. He rocked between River's hands, body singing, screaming for him to just get on with it, and Simon let loose one short, sharp cry when the first rough pulse of his sac had River's mouth moving, dropping over his tip again. The hand that had been wrapped around Simon's cock was suddenly on his spit-slicked balls, just like that, rolling them, pressing, pushing just enough that Simon couldn't even hold his head up.

Eyes closed, head lolling back, Simon gasped as he came in the wet, warm cavern of River's mouth, suction there again as River swallowed around him.

"Bloody...*fucking* hell." It was a groan, but that was fine. It was also forced from Simon's mouth by the impact of his body dropping onto the mattress below Morgan's feet. And River was still kneeling, looking pleased as fuck and licking his lips.

"Dude." Yeah, a bloody fucking pleased look on River's face. Smug-like, really. Then again, Simon figured the bloke had reason. "Way better than tasting rubbers." River's nose wrinkled just a bit and Simon had to fight to keep from saying just how cute that was. "I don't care what they say, man, even the flavoured ones don't taste anything like mint or banana or whatever the fuck."

Morgan laughed, the sound shaky and thin, and when Simon managed to turn his head, yeah. His bloke was still stroking, still running a big hand up and down that beautiful hard shaft. Seeping already, Morgan's cock was dark, looked almost angry in a way. "Si tastes way better than anything else, Riv." Oh, a full bloody sentence. Impressive, considering how hard Morgan was breathing. "Sometimes think I could live on just his cum. Oh, fuck."

Those last words were likely in response to the way River was licking his lips again when Simon looked. It was different, somehow. Like River was still tasting Simon there but was wondering how Morgan's flavour would compare. Of course, Simon told himself with a silent, breathless laugh, that was likely because River's eyes were locked on Morgan's cock. "Now, now, love," Simon murmured, mostly for River, though he made sure Morgan could hear him, too. "Taste a right treat, yourself. All musky and bittersweet. Made a meal of you more than once."

Yeah, that was it. Prod River. Push him to what he already wanted to do. Then Simon would do what *he* wanted to do, even if he wasn't quite up for it yet. He would be. And probably soon, because River was on the bed the second Simon shifted to lie beside Morgan. Ass in the air, elbows down on the bed between Morgan's thighs, River was bloody well stunning, and the more so for the obvious desire on his face.

Simon watched, bit back a groan as the tongue that had tormented him so nicely flicked out, danced over Morgan's tip, then slipped back into River's mouth. A soft hum came next and River grinned, eyes sparkling. "Simon's right, man," River said, his voice bubbling like he was trying not to laugh. "You taste different. But just as good. Fuck, should have done this sooner." Then Simon watched as that mouth opened, tongue swirling over Morgan's thick, round tip again, and when River closed his lips around Morgan's cock, cheeks hollowing a bit as he gave that first experimental suck Simon remembered so well from minutes earlier, Morgan moaned.

It was a deep sound, rich and full, and went straight to Simon's balls. So much stronger than the thready sound of Morgan's words of moments before. And River groaned or something, something Simon couldn't define that might have been a word had it not been uttered around heavy, hot flesh. It didn't matter what it was. Didn't make a bit of difference, because yeah. He'd seen River suck Morgan's cock before, many a time. Never without rubber between mouth and skin, though, and knowing how good it was, Simon found it even more arousing than ever, as unlikely as that seemed even to him.

It was likely what Morgan had felt, watching River on Simon's prick, though the amazing part was that Morgan was still hard; hadn't blown his wad whilst watching. It was an affecting sight, after all. Enough to have Simon's recently spent cock twitching, filling slowly, and River. Bloody River was still there, bent over, taking Morgan in, long hair draping down to the side away from Simon. Like a backdrop of variegated yellow silk, framing the slow, careful slide of pink lips on olive skin, River's mouth pushing down to meet Morgan's fingers where Morgan still held his own dick.

"You look bloody gorgeous, love," Simon said then, looking up, meeting Morgan's wide brown eyes. "Our boy, sucking you bare, and you just...so hot, Morgan. So fucking stunning." A tiny whine answered him, and Simon grinned. Non-verbal was good. Better than good.

It could get better still, though. Would, if Simon had a say in the matter. Which he did, he thought with a smirk. In fact, with River's mouth so full and Morgan sunk deep in sensation, Simon was the only one who did have any say. And Simon said, silently and solely to himself, that River should be getting something out of it all, too. And if that meant Simon got another shuddering, blissful orgasm out of the deal, well, he'd somehow manage to suffer through.

Lube, right there on the table by the bed. Condoms, too, because unprotected blowjobs were one thing, but full-on sex would require a bit of a chat before going without. Then Simon moved, slid down a little, eyes on River's hot little mouth taking in Morgan's big, fat cock, and yeah. Bloody fucking amazing, just to see that.

Fingers slick, wet with cool gel, pushed slowly between River's cheeks, and River barely paused, just opened his legs, and that was nice. Beyond nice, it was sodding brilliant. Tight little hole, still just as tight as that first time Simon had touched it, even after months of Simon and Morgan opening it up. Fucking perfect. And tight as River was, his body still let Simon in, two fingers going deep, like River didn't care about a little burn, a bit of sting.

Well, maybe he didn't, Simon decided, or maybe he liked it, because yeah, River was moving faster on Morgan then. Mouth pushing down, one hand pulling Morgan's away as River pushed down more, took in more thick, hard flesh. And Morgan was grunting, arching just a bit against the sheets, whining and gripping the bed linens now that both hands were free.

Yeah, Simon didn't blame him. Hard to resist grabbing River's hair, forcing that lovely mouth all the way down, and Morgan was so big, he'd do River some damage if that happened. The sheets might never recover, but far better them than River.

He moved his own fingers too. Slid them in and out of River's ass, pushing apart, pulling together as Simon twisted his wrist and added one more digit. Bloody fucking Christ, he always managed to forget just how good River felt inside. Like his mind couldn't retain the sensation in memory or some such. The same happened with Morgan though, so Simon figured it was just his way.

River was moaning, Simon could hear it. Moaning and rocking, lips taking another inch of Morgan's hot cock, River's ass pushing back each time he pulled his mouth up a bit, and yeah. Yeah, that was bloody perfect. Simon's cock thought so too, bobbing and full as it was.

"Hold on, pet," Simon ordered as he pulled his fingers from River's slicked bum to open the packet and roll latex over himself. "Might even want to hold my bloke's hips. Likely to be a rough ride, this." Because yeah, it for damned sure would be. Morgan's cock all bare in River's mouth, the sounds both of his men were making? Yeah. Rough and hard and sodding long, for that matter. Second go for him, after all, meaning Simon would last a bit.

He waited long enough to see River take him at his word, the one blue eye Simon could see going darker while River levered himself a bit, lifted just enough to get his hands settled firmly on the mattress, elbows bent to leave him free to suck as he chose. And yeah. The bed was better for support, judging from the way Morgan was moving. "Fuck, honey," Morgan managed, sounding strained and near-breathless. "Fucking fuck."

"That's the plan, love," Simon answered with a wink he thought was lost on his bloke. And he moved, got to his knees and shifted down, around, right behind River, behind golden skin and long, strong thighs and shimmering slick hole. "Now," Simon added, his hands finding skin, gripping and fastening tight as he pressed forward, pushed inside, covered tip breaching before sinking deep. "Fucking hell. Tight, pet." Always so bloody tight.

River made some sort of sound, mouth still full of cock, and Simon felt himself grinning, even as he pulled himself fully from the tightness surrounding him, then drove back inside. Yeah. Like that. Bloody perfect. Again would be even better. Long, slow withdrawal, one hand leaving River's skin to hold the edge of the rubber as he pressed tip to hole and jabbed deep, pushing another of those sounds out of River and around Morgan's cock. Morgan felt it, too, because yeah. "Fuck!" Yelped, sounding stunned, shocked, what-sodding-ever.

Again, and River's head popped up. "Can't breathe when you do that," but it wasn't really a complaint because River was pushing back and his head went down again and Morgan moaned loud and long, so…one more time, completely out, then another long, hard slam to flush, Simon's hand moving back to River, back to a smooth hip, to soft skin over flexing muscle and hard bone.

Perfect, all of it. River's hole holding him, squeezing and relaxing every time Simon moved. Morgan gasping, grunting, still arching under them, pushing up into River's mouth. River's long, golden spine, moving in undulating waves as the bloke tried to pay attention to them both, because River was clearly giving as good as he got. Morgan was making that more than clear.

Then "Oh, fuck. Fuck!" from Morgan, moving his big hands from the sheets to grasp River's head, and River was making that little choking noise that had so alarmed Simon the first time he'd heard it, but he'd since come to know was a good sound. And River pulling up, sinking down again, and Simon knew he was doing that thing with his tongue, because Morgan…bloody fuck if Morgan didn't look like he'd just found his own bit of Heaven. Eyes rolled back, head back against the wall, looking bloody well debauched and about to go mad, Morgan was almost unbearably gorgeous.

Simon moved harder, faster, pistoning deep and rough, and River grunted every time their sacs met, skin slapping, the sounds right there under Morgan's strained whining moans, and yeah. Yeah, just like that.

Morgan, letting loose one sharp shout. Simon's hand moving under River, gripping the bloke's long, thin cock and pulling. River bucking back, meeting Simon's next hard thrust, tight little hole going tighter still, and Simon was done. Was finished and coming, throbbing, spilling hard and long into latex while River's dick spurted in Simon's hand. River swallowed everything Morgan offered up so willingly, head still moving some, still bobbing for another moment or three, then stopping.

Sweaty flesh slipped a little, slid as Simon pulled himself from River's body; as River relinquished his hold on Morgan's spent cock. And when they wrapped together, a pile of limp, sodden bodies, Simon chuckled, soft and low. "Bloody brilliant, loves," he murmured against Morgan's shoulder.

"Dude," River answered from Morgan's other side, "that fucking kicked ass. We so need to do that again. It was fucking awesome."

"Fucking awesome," Morgan said, too, his words mixing with River's last, and Simon chuckled again at the harmony.

"Bloody right," Simon agreed, stifling a yawn. "Sodding good with your mouth, pet. And your bum."

His chuckle was contagious, Simon realised; so was the yawn, apparently, but that wasn't a bad thing. Nap, he decided, then they'd get back to it. Hours still before he and Morgan would have to hare off for their own rooms. Best to wear River out before then so the bloke wouldn't even notice them going. More importantly, so River wouldn't notice how hard it was to walk away, even for the night.

* * * *

New Game, this time in Prague, and something about the way Patrice was briefing them told Morgan that he wasn't going to like it. The woman was usually straight up, gave them the step-by-step, then sent them on their merry way. She didn't approach things daintily. Patrice wasn't a dainty kind of woman, for all that she was petite and ladylike. The fact that she was sneaking around verbally this time was a little bit disturbing. No. A lot.

Simon felt it too, if the slowly hardening expression on his face was any indication, and it was. Morgan knew that much. Simon had never had much patience for bullshit, after all, and when it came to Patrice, *not much* became *none*. Which Morgan was sure Patrice already knew, and that only made everything that much worse. Maybe. If she ever got to the fucking point, he'd know for sure.

"Cern Oblocha Bar is rather well known in the city amongst a certain clientele," she was saying, and thank fucking Christ. A name, even of a bar, though Morgan still didn't know where it was. Prague was a big damned place. "Unfortunately, you won't be able to run River and Moon as a team this time. The client's target isn't even remotely interested in women."

Okay, that explained it, Morgan decided. They always ran River and his sister together. They had that weird twin thing going on most of the time, which made them an incredibly effective team. Not this time, though.

"River can't go in without back-up." Morgan said it bluntly, but he wanted to make that much entirely clear. No matter how many people they had scattered in whatever the fuck sized bar it was, River was for damned sure going to have a partner within arm's length, right up until the fucking *fucking* portion of the Game began. Even then, they would be listening. Or Simon would, though Morgan usually shared that duty. Not this time. This time, if Morgan had anything to say about it, *he* would be River's back-up and Moon could man the comm, coordinate the rest of the team with Simon, in case an extraction was needed.

Simon still looked hard when Morgan gave him a glance, though one of those brown brows rose. "Think the bint knows that already, love," he said, but his eyes were still on Patrice. "Something more going on here than changing our bloody line-up, yeah?"

Well, Simon would know. He spent more time with the woman than Morgan did. "Okay...so it might be a good idea to just say it," Morgan suggested quickly. "You know, so Simon doesn't decide to shoot you and

I don't have to help hide the body." And yeah, he was kidding. Mostly. "Now would be good." He could sound reasonable. He did.

Patrice sighed softly, almost silently, but then she nodded, the gesture sharp and sudden, like she'd just made a decision or something. "All right. This particular Game is somewhat outside your team's usual operational parameters but we don't have another available unit that's convincing enough to achieve the necessary proximity."

Her voice went on, though Morgan wasn't paying attention to her words, but to what they meant. Yeah, Patrice had had good reason to be skating around the truth. She wasn't sending them out to acquire or disseminate information. It wasn't that sort of a Game. In fact, it was a snatch and grab, the target to be delivered to a certain group that wasn't known for its kind and gentle nature.

"You're asking my lot to kill a man," Simon said before Morgan could even formulate his feelings into words. "Might be someone else what pulls the bloody trigger, but you're looking to River to make it happen." Well, that pretty much summed it up...and Morgan thought he should care more than he did.

Oh, he cared that Patrice actually wanted River to be a part of it. Snatching someone the Russian fucking Mob couldn't get their hands on from a club that same Mob couldn't get inside didn't sound like a walk in the park, and River... Fuck if Morgan was sure the kid had it in him. Fuck if he was going to risk his and Simon's lover on someone who'd pissed off a bunch of thugs enough that said thugs were willing to pay the FGC just to get them access. Whoever it was, he had to be competition or something. Part of a rival faction, stepping on toes that should have been danced around rather than trampled over.

"I'll handle that part," Morgan heard himself saying, but that was fine. He'd been responsible, both directly and indirectly, for more than one person dying in the past. He could handle it. River probably could, too, but Morgan doubted that it wouldn't leave a mark on the young man's spirit and heart. "Get in, get whoever the fuck the target is to take me somewhere, and the rest of the team hits us in transit. We deliver the fucker to an agreed-upon location, and we're out."

Simon didn't look happy about that idea at all, but Morgan tried to let his determination show in his gaze and apparently Simon got it because he frowned. Shook his head. Frowned more. Finally nodded. Slowly, but Simon nodded, and Morgan figured Simon had just worked out what being point on the new Game would likely do to River, too. "Still can't believe you're asking us to do this, you dozy mare." More growl than comment, but whatever. Simon was on board.

Patrice crossed her arms and gave them a look, first Morgan, then Simon. Morgan doubted it was any more pleasant when it got to Simon than it had been for him, what with Patrice and Simon's weird adversarial friendship. Possibly less.

"It's not a request." Patrice's voice was flat. Blunt. "I've assigned your team to this Game and I expect you and your people to complete it to the best of your ability, Simon. That's why you're here. Because you're a Gentleman and in charge of running the only team that is likely to accomplish the client's goal. It isn't optional or open to discussion. Now, I believe Marcus has already sent the pertinent data to your rooms.

Familiarise yourselves and brief your team. You leave tomorrow evening; the time is in the file."

Simon glared. Morgan saw that much before his own glare fell on the woman. But they both for damned sure got up and left the room, though Morgan paused and glanced back. His eyes widened just a bit and he reached out, took Simon's hand and squeezed lightly.

"She doesn't like this any more than we do," he murmured, hopefully pitching his voice to a softness that the ever-present surveillance systems wouldn't pick up. "I think it's come from the Director, Si." He really did. Because when he'd looked back, Morgan had seen Patrice, still standing but leaning on the table, one hand holding her up while the other was fisted beside it, her head bowed as though she was tired. Weary.

"Don't give a dog's bloody bollocks," Simon answered just as softly; just as grating as Morgan expected. "We do this job, love, and I'm through with the bitch. Would take you, our bloke, petal *and* the sodding wee chits and blokes out of here if I could, too. Can't, but I can bloody fucking well refuse to work with that bint again."

Shit. Just shit. Simon was right. Including the kids, that would be nine. There wasn't a single fucking chance of getting them all out, and Rico would never agree to leave the other kids behind and... "Fuck. We'll work it out, Si. We'll have to." Because Morgan wasn't actually willing to leave, either. He hadn't realised it until just that moment, but there it was.

The Club had taken them in, him and Rico. And Morgan had known what he was signing on for, no matter that he'd fucking waffled right at first. The FGC had made the run to destroy NovoTech's medical research programme, and it was that very Game that had made Rico safe. That kept her that way, too. He owed the FGC. And sure, the Club did things that were questionable from a so-called moral standpoint, but so did the government.

And they didn't know *why* the Russians wanted the guy at the Cern Oblacha Bar, but if criminals were willing to pay top dollar to get their hands on another criminal, Morgan couldn't find it in himself to be upset about it.

He still thought that when he and Simon had read the fucking file. Thought it even more, really. The Cern Oblacha Bar had once been known as *the* place to find and rent pretty young things for a night or two. Then the guy they'd been pointed at—nobody knew who he was, there were no pictures; not even a name—somehow had swept in and taken over, ousted the front men running the place for the Russians. Then some of the hustlers and whores had started disappearing, while electronic hacking and the small bit of surveillance the Russians had managed showed very large influxes of Czech crowns into the nightclub's accounts. That those amounts coincided so closely with the disappearances seemed telling.

"The bloody fucking bastard is selling them off," Simon said as he scrolled back and re-read what little intel they had. "This piece of shit we're to grab. He's gone from being a bloody pimp to selling people like cattle."

Well, yeah. "That's what it looks like, honey," Morgan answered, nodding as he read over Simon's shoulder. "I wonder..." He frowned, then pulled his internal comm from his pocket, pressing a few buttons quickly, calling through to IT. "Jensen, it's Morgan. Can you do me a favour? Hack in to the Czech police files. See if there's been a sudden increase in the number of 'unidentified bodies' found in and around Prague for the last…" He looked at Simon.

Simon nodded sharply and scrolled again. "Eight months, love. Looks like that's when our daft rotter took over."

"Eight months," Morgan repeated. "I have a feeling this fucker we're after is even worse than it seems." He paused, then outlined what he hoped were decent search parameters. Young. Attractive before death, though that might not be apparent after. Signs of sexual assault or long-term physical abuse. Short-term, too. "See if there are any links to Cern Oblacha Bar, okay? Even rumours, though something verified would be better. Thanks, man."

He ended the comm call and frowned as Simon closed the file on the computer. "He'll get back to us in a couple hours, Si. I guess we should brief the team, huh?"

Fuck, the Game really was outside their usual kind of thing, but Morgan was actually looking forward to it, all of a sudden, because if they were right—their target had earned a fucking ass-kicking the likes of which had never been seen. Morgan had a sneaking suspicion that the Russian Mob would see to it that the fucker got it, too. Right before they put a bullet in the shithead's brain.

"Yeah. Yeah, love," Simon answered as he pushed away from the computer. "Might even owe bitchy-bitch an apology. You know. In my head. Would never say so to the bint's face, of course."

Well, duh, Morgan thought, pulling Simon in for a tight, hard hug. And maybe he owed a silent apology, too. Because maybe the fucking pose he'd seen Patrice in when he'd looked back had been worry, concern for their team. Maybe Patrice had been dreading the possible — probable, Morgan admitted silently, considering the information in the file — loss of at least one of their team, especially if she'd been ordered by the Director to accept the Game in the first place. It wouldn't be River, though. Or Simon. Morgan would do everything he could to make sure of that.

It didn't take Jensen the couple of hours the man had estimated. It took less than one before Morgan's comm unit buzzed in his pocket. He frowned slightly, then nodded at Simon before stepping to the back of the briefing room to take the call.

No pictures, but Morgan didn't mind hearing that. He might be comfortable with dealing death when it was deserved, but that didn't mean he had any great love of seeing the fucking outcome. Still, eleven bodies in eight months. Bodies that fit the parameters, according to Jensen. No one over twenty-five, all in good physical shape, and all fucking dead. Some minor signs of drug use, yes, but nothing that would or had been responsible for the deaths. Five shot in various body parts, two drowned. The other four appeared to have been literally beaten to death, though whoever had done it had left little evidence behind. Shit.

Morgan thanked Jensen quickly then returned to the front of the room. "We're on," he told Simon bluntly, then Morgan leant back against the wall while Simon added the new intel to the briefing. He watched while the team's faces closed, grew hard. Even River seemed to shut down, his lips compressing into a thin line while Moon's eyes narrowed to sapphire slits, small circles of red appearing on her cheeks.

"Right, then," Simon said when he'd finished sharing the details, "we're international on this one, so we're going in naked. Nothing. Not a single bloody ceramic knife or carbon fibre anything. Last thing we need is to have even one of us come under suspicion on arrival. We've an armoury in Prague, under cover of a tourist shop. The address will be in your personal packets. River, you're with Morgan on this Game. Hook and Thorn, second-in team. Moon, you're with me. Now head off to your bloody beds, yeah? I see even one yawn tomorrow, it won't go well for you."

Simon held it together until the team had filed out, though River seemed to know something was up because he lingered for a moment until Morgan shook his head. Then River followed the others and Morgan pushed away from the wall, raising his hands to rest on Simon's tense shoulders.

"They're gone, honey," Morgan murmured against one pale ear. "And it'll be fine. We'll get it fucking done and haul ass right back here."

A sigh left Simon when Morgan pressed his thumbs deep into tight muscle. "I don't like this, love," Simon muttered back, clearly trying to avoid being overheard just as much as Morgan was. "Been a year since Thorn and Hook played a *real* Game. Our bloke and his sis? Never. Bloody well worries me, yeah?"

"Yeah," Morgan answered, biting his lip for a second. "I'm not really fucking thrilled myself. We need to work out some new protocols, Si. And...maybe you'll tell me the rest of why this one freaks you out. It's not just because of the team." It wasn't. Morgan knew that much, though he was pretty sure no one else did. No one else knew Simon as well as Morgan did, though; not even River. "Come on, honey," he added as he stepped back, letting his hands drop from Simon's tense body. "Let's get back to our rooms and dissect the fucking file. I want to know everything possible about what the fuck we're walking into."

Chapter Ten

Man, the Prague job was a bitch. And not in the fun, spanky way, either. The clothes were fun, though.

Tight. Black. Shiny. Yeah, those described the pants River was wearing pretty well. Not leather, but some weird-ass stuff like the chick from the Matrix would wear. And laces. All down the outside of his legs until the pants disappeared into the tops of silver-studded boots.

"I kind of think it's a little bit much, dude," he said, giving Morgan a grin in the mirror, because yeah. He looked hot, but whatever the pants were made of was thin. So thin, there wasn't a single doubt that anyone looking would be able to tell River was circumcised with a single glance.

Morgan met his eyes in the reflective glass, the brown stare so deep River thought he could feel it like a touch. Or his cock could, anyway. "I think you're gonna look fucking obscene in about a minute, baby," Morgan answered, and oh. Oh, hell yeah. River did like that little growl. It went straight from his ears to his balls and lingered there, rough velvet and smooth steel. "Yeah...not even a minute."

Well, fuck him if Morgan wasn't right, River saw when he looked at himself again. Black shirt, open almost to the top of the pants, and...okay. Not a single question of whether anyone would be able to tell he was hard. Not with the tight-as-shit pants. "Dude. I think I need to keep these for when we get back home." Simon would probably throw him down and fuck him hard, River figured, and that was just more incentive.

Morgan snorted and shook his head, but River saw him in the mirror. Saw one big hand adjusting the front of leather pants. "You'll be lucky if I don't rip them off you before we even make it to the fucking club, Riv. Now move your ass. Work to do."

That reminded him and River turned, glancing over his shoulder to check out his butt in the shiny-as-fuck whatever-the-hell pants. Yeah, no doubt that he was naked underneath. No doubt that the way the material dipped into his crack and moulded to him looked like an invitation, which was pretty much the point.

"Cool. Get it done, then..." River waggled his brows, laughing when Morgan groaned. "You look damn good too, man," he offered as Morgan turned away, heading for the door. It was true, too. Morgan could rock leather in ways River hadn't even imagined. Leather pants, leather vest worn open, no shirt. Bronze nipples just flashing out every now and then. Yeah. The dude was fucking awesome. And his, River reminded himself with a grin. Or sort of. For the moment, anyway.

There was something a little bit strange about walking down the street with Morgan, no Simon in sight. It felt a little off, but River could deal. Had to. It was a Game, after all. And maybe the odd part was that it wasn't Moon with him, River decided. Maybe it was just that he wasn't used to being on point with anyone but his sister. They were more than siblings; more than twins, after all. Moony was his best friend, too. They'd trained together under their dad's tutelage while growing up. They'd been working runs together since day one with the Club, too, and they for damn sure knew each other's rhythms.

Of course, he also knew Morgan's rhythms. River smirked and put a little rock in his walk. He knew just about everything there was to know about Morgan's rhythms. Simon's too. Different thing, sure, but whatever. None of which was helping his cock lose interest in trying to give a wave every time Morgan took a step.

They were already sort of established at the Cern Oblocha Bar. Four nights in a row, he and Morgan had gone there. Visiting from the States, blah-blah-blah, loving the nightlife. Not a single hint that River spoke Czech because it was always useful to hear what people were saying when they thought the subject of their words didn't understand.

The fifth night started out just the same as the rest. He and Morgan headed for the bar, getting drinks and tossing them back. Then dancing, throwing themselves into the teeming mass of people on the third floor. River wasn't the biggest Techo fan ever, but he could deal. Any time he could rub up against Morgan was a good thing, especially with the way his slick pants tried to cling to Morgan's leather.

Morgan could actually dance, too, which shouldn't have surprised him considering the way Morgan fought and fucked, but there it was. River had been nearly stunned on their first night at the bar. Not enough to break cover and show it, but yeah. Morgan had known. Still did, judging by the smug little quirk at the corners of his lips that just made River hotter.

So, dancing. Grinding against each other, much like the rest of the people around them were doing. And all the while, River imagined he could feel eyes watching him, watching *them*. Not regular eyes, but hopefully the eyes of the fucker they were there for. The guy who hid on the very private, very secure balcony area above the third floor and behind the chrome and glass railing. Up there at the top of the stairs that were guarded by four guys who looked like they'd been in more than their share of fights and who were clearly armed if someone knew what to look for.

"Come on, baby," Morgan shouted from maybe two inches away, and River barely heard him. "Let's get another drink!" River just nodded and let Morgan take his hand, following the man's winding path through drunken revellers who might have fallen over were it not for the press of bodies holding them mostly upright.

Five nights, and it was almost time. Minutes, maybe, before Morgan took the next step in the plan they'd all agreed on. River didn't like it, but yeah. With any luck, it would work. He hoped. They all hoped.

It felt like they'd spent an eternity getting to the bar, but the crowd had nearly doubled in size from when he and Morgan had arrived, or maybe it was just that the two lower floors were playing crap music. Whatever the reason, River was actually starting to worry that the fight they had planned would be lost in the madness; that it wouldn't garner them the kind of attention it needed to. He arched a questioning look at Morgan when they finally shored up against chrome, bodies squeezed between so many others desperately in search of a bit of liquid relief, or maybe just liquid.

Morgan's frown was barely there, but River saw it before it disappeared under shouted words to the nearest bartender. He moved his hands on Morgan's body, sliding under the open vest, pinching already tight nipples almost roughly because yeah. River wasn't about to pass on the opportunity. Not when it had Morgan's hips rocking against him like that. Even so, he stuck with the plan, pushing his ass back against whoever was behind him and letting his eyes close when a hand that clearly wasn't Morgan's came from behind, snaked around his waist and down to cover his still-hard cock in the shiny-as-shit pants. Making a bid for what River seemed to be offering, just like they'd known would happen. It was that kind of a club.

Morgan pretended not to notice right at first, just like they'd planned. He paid the guy behind the bar, then started to hand a plastic cup to River, and man, Morgan could do jealous at the drop of a hat. If River hadn't known it was a set-up, he would have been worried.

"You little fucking slut!" Yeah, that was it. Loud and pissed and audible even over the music. "Fucking whore! What the fuck! I took you away from all that shit and the first chance you get, you're ready to fucking spread for any piece of shit who touches you! Fuck!"

River made himself sneer, made a smug and nasty little smile spread his lips as he pushed against the hand that was still on him, still cupping him through slick and tight. "Like it's my fault you won't fuck me!" He yelled the words, rocking his hips between the strange hand and the equally unknown groin of whoever was touching him. Male, because River could feel hardness right up against his ass. "You knew what I was when you brought me here, you asshole! I can't wait forever, just hoping you'll get over your fucking fear of fucking a guy!"

Morgan's backhand didn't really hurt. Hell, it was more sound than fury, just hard enough to pull blood to the surface of River's cheek. Even then, he could see the apology, the self-loathing hidden deep in Morgan's eyes. Man, it was disturbing seeing even that much. Fuck if River didn't want to kiss the man, but that would ruin their Play, damn it. So he laughed.

He laughed again, louder still, and shook his head, nasty little smile going heated, River hoped. "Now you're getting it. Do it again and maybe you'll relax enough to fuck. You know you want to. You like it. Like hitting me. Well, I like it too. Do it! One more time and I'll probably come right here!" The anonymous hand on him moved then, gripping River's cock right through his pants and the cock behind him got even harder, which was fucking gross. He was playing a part, but River had never really understood pain-sluts. A little slap and tickle was one thing, but getting off on being beaten just didn't make anything like sense to him. It obviously turned on the dude behind him, though.

"You sick fucking bitch!" Yeah, Morgan looked disgusted, all right. So much that River really hoped he was still Playing. "You want to fuck? Fine! Let's fuck!" One more backhand and Morgan grabbed him, dragging River roughly through the crowd of people who were just standing there. Just watching. Dragging River away from whoever had been feeling him up, thank God.

River didn't know how Morgan managed it, but a path seemed to open for them. Maybe Morgan still looked as disgusted, as dangerous, as he'd looked by the bar. Whatever it was, though...man! People couldn't seem to get out of the way fast enough. They were down on the first floor and heading out through the nightclub's front door in minutes.

The doorman stopped them, one beefy hand in the centre of Morgan's chest, a bored look on the man's rough face. "Your whore must know to behave or you do not enter here," he said in heavily accented English and Morgan snorted.

"He'll be lucky if I let him out in public again after tonight." Morgan's tone was sneering enough that River couldn't help blinking, worrying just a little bit that Morgan meant it. Man. But the doorman was nodding and muttering in a way that told River he was wired in to the bar's security, though the Czech words weren't clear enough to make out more than "pretty slut" and "punish". Then Morgan was stalking down the street, pulling River along by the arm like it was a leash.

"We made a fucking impression," Morgan announced after sweeping their hotel room for bugs and not finding any that weren't their own. "We're in for the night."

Talking to Simon, River figured, though he'd taken his own ear bud out as soon as they'd closed their door. Man. Fucking messed up night, even with knowing what was coming. More messed up that, even with knowing it was all an act, he'd enjoyed Morgan's possessiveness. Enjoyed the false fury at seeing someone else touching River. He was so totally screwed. River knew it, even as he sat on the edge of the bed, shiny pants and all.

"Yeah," Morgan said next, and when River looked Morgan was leaning against the dresser, eyes closed as those big hands scrubbed through short brown hair. "Yeah, I know, Si. It still felt..." A pause and silent nod, then "Yeah," again. "No, he's fine. Better than... Yeah. You're right. I will. Fuck, I want to. As long as you know... Okay. Me too, honey. Tomorrow. Not too early. I'll probably be up for...yeah. I know, it's just... Okay. Night, Si."

Morgan pulled the bud from his ear, eyes still closed, and River tried to relax. He was still nearly vibrating, though. Tense, like they were still in Play, rather than finished with the act and in the relative safety of their hotel room. Maybe because Morgan still looked so tight, River decided. Those strong, broad shoulders were drawn up, hunched into hard knots of muscle where the vest didn't cover them. Shit.

"Dude. That whole thing was..." he started, but Morgan's eyes opened, pinned him to the bed. Stole the breath from his lungs with heat and, yeah, a good bit of that fury from before, which apparently wasn't as fake as River had thought.

"Get out of those fucking clothes and get your ass in the shower," Morgan ordered. Snarled. Whatever. "Now."

Dude. Wicked. Hot. Almost scary, except River liked it. Was starting to think maybe it wasn't just him who was feeling more than casually attached. He was starting to think it while he peeled the black, plastic-like pants down his legs and kicked out of the boots, though, because one thing River was entirely sure of was that Morgan was serious. Seriously intent and borderline growling, which only had River moving faster.

Pants, boots, socks, shirt. Then yeah, right to the shower because Morgan was staring, glaring, doing some shit with just his eyes that had River shivering. Danger there, in Morgan's eyes, closer to the surface than at the nightclub, even, which was sort of wild, but sort of cool, too.

It didn't take much to shift the lever in the tile enclosure; didn't take more than a thought to step inside. Not hot yet, but not really cold either. Sort of...oh. Okay, hot. Yeah. Fuck. Almost too hot, River realised, his skin shuddering in that weird-ass in-between place where too hot and too cold were confused. He found the lever again, only to be stopped by Morgan's hand. Bigger, stronger, darker than his own, that hand wrapped over his, Morgan's grip tight. Demanding.

"Leave it." Words grunted like Morgan was trying to hold them in but couldn't. Man. Hotter than the water. Then Morgan was pressed up behind him, muscles and skin and long, heavy cock right there in his crease, tip up on River's lower back. "How's your face?"

River blinked, frowned, shook his head as he tried to figure out what Morgan was talking about and...oh, right. His cheek. He'd already forgotten. "It's fine, man. Not even red anymore." He couldn't see it, hadn't bothered with a mirror since they'd got back, but he could tell. No warmth or heat that wasn't caused by the damned hot water or Morgan up against him.

"Good." That was all. No sorry or anything, just good. Then better because Morgan released River's fingers and that muscled, lightly haired forearm was around River's waist, holding him against hard flesh, his spine to Morgan's chest. "Stay," Morgan added and River could only nod while that arm moved away, adjusted the water just a little, heat going from almost unbearable to something slightly less sharp.

Gel from the bottle of liquid soap that River liked, and lather, suds, strong hands careful as they moved over River's body in long strokes that weren't gentle but missed being too firm by just a hair. "Man," River moaned, head tilted back onto Morgan's shoulder, Morgan's soft lips full and open on his neck. "Morgan. Dude. Yeah." There was nothing else to say. Nothing that wouldn't break whatever the hell it was Morgan was doing. Whatever it was, River liked it. Wanted more of it.

He barely held back a whine when Morgan pushed him away, but those hands merely turned him, tipped River's head back until his hair became wet, a heavy curtain down his back, rinsing smoke and sweat away. And Morgan was still touching him, touching River's skin like that was his purpose in life. Like Morgan's fingers had been made solely for just that. Then Morgan's hands moved, gripped his ass, and River moaned. Moaned into Morgan's mouth because it was right there on his, open and hot and tasting faintly of gin but mostly just tasting of Morgan.

Tongues and teeth, and wasn't that just perfect. Man, he would have worried about getting used to it, but River knew he already was. Morgan's mouth, and Simon's. Yeah, both of them were on the short list of things River didn't want to think about doing without. But Simon wasn't there at the moment, he reminded himself. Just him and Morgan, which felt kind of weird and a little bit dirty, in the good way. And hot. Fuck if it wasn't hotter than even the water, somehow.

The soap should have stung when Morgan moved two slick fingers to River's hole and pushed them deep. River spared a brief moment of thought to admitting it should have, and maybe it would later, but right then it felt good. Perfect. Just enough slip and slide to ease things, but not so much that he didn't feel the soft burn. Five nights they'd been in Prague, keeping up their cover, and they hadn't fucked even once. That was about to change, River knew, and thank God for that. He'd stroked off more in those days than he'd done in months.

"Fuck, yeah," River heard himself gasping against Morgan's cheek, the skin smooth, still clear of stubble from the shaving before the nightclub. "Man, that's..." The word perfect ran through River's mind but didn't make it past his lips because Morgan was pulling away, pulling back, and that sucked. Sucked more than River could ever manage to articulate. Then Morgan was back, River's conditioner in one hand, and okay. Better. Much better for thick fingers to push that into him than soap. "Oh, fuck."

"In a minute," Morgan's reply came out on a groaned breath, fumbling with the flip-top on the bottle, getting it open. Then a viscous, spurting sound that would have been funny any other time but at the moment only served to have River's cock jumping, finishing the short road to full and hard and leaking.

His eyes closed as Morgan's fingers opened him again, sank deep and moved, and River wasn't sure which of them gasped louder when Morgan dropped the bottle and pulled one of River's legs up, holding his knee at Morgan's waist. "Morgan." Just that. Morgan. Nothing else, but River figured the little whine was doing the begging for him. The whine in his voice and his hips, because he was for damned sure rocking, body begging just as much as his tone, trying everything it could manage to get those thick digits deeper.

"Riv. Fuck, Riv." Morgan sounded just as needy, as fucking wanton as River was. Sounded it and was, River realised, because damn, those fingers were gone and a small dip on Morgan's part later, River was up on the toes of the foot that was still on the shower floor. Morgan's cock was right there, wet with water and hotter than fuck, pressing at him, pushing at his hole, so different from feeling latex. "Okay, baby? Fuck, tell me it's okay…"

"Fucking awesome." The familiar words left River's lips before he'd even had time to think, but it didn't matter. He figured he would have said the same even if he'd taken an hour to consider it. And Morgan was moaning, sounding relieved and just as possessive as he'd seemed earlier, and that was good. Fucking perfect. More perfect when Morgan's hand tightened on River's leg, holding it up, while the other took his hip, pulling River down onto the blunt heat that was no less forceful for the lack of sharpness.

"Oh. Oh, man…" River was pretty sure he sounded stunned, but fuck if he wasn't. Thick. Fucking hot. Somehow smoother than ever before. And man, he needed to buy stock in the company that made his fucking conditioner because the stuff was just working with River's ass, letting him spread almost easily around Morgan's tip. And then Morgan was in, fat bulb pushing deep, hefty shaft spearing up and in and oh, man. So fucking full. So damned good.

River's eyes opened, caught Morgan's. Caught fierce pride and some sort of smug certainty in that dark gaze that River couldn't even pretend to dislike. Even so, "Dude. You drop me, your dick is gonna break off in my ass." He had to say it. Anything to keep himself from going off like a rocket with Morgan inside him for less than a minute.

Morgan chuckled, though the sound was thin, like Morgan was only holding on by the same hair's breadth. "I won't fucking drop you, baby. Never fucking drop you, Riv." And if River read more into those words than Morgan meant, well, no need to share, was there? "Hold on," Morgan ordered and River found his arms wrapping around Morgan's neck, around those strong damned shoulders. A shift, a small bend, and both of River's legs were around Morgan's waist, that long, thick cock in him up to the hilt, and man. Oh, man.

Water, off. Moving, and hard flesh rocking in River's ass, then they were on the bed, Morgan laying them both down, still deep, so damned deep. And so naked inside him, River reminded himself, though the heat alone made the thought unnecessary. Then Morgan had River's hair, still wet, dripping, spread over the pillows at the head of the bed.

"Man. Fuck," and he was surprised he'd managed that much. But Morgan nodded, pulled back, hands on the bed beside River's shoulders, and River's own hands were at Morgan's nipples though River didn't know when he'd moved them.

Long, slow thrusts that pushed and pulled sounds from both of them and River couldn't help thinking that Simon could hear them, that the whole team could, though he was sure Moon had bowed out once the shower had started running, just like he did when she was on point. But Simon would hear them, would be listening, and River wondered if the man knew about the rubber he and Morgan weren't using. But Morgan's mouth was on his again and River lost the thought in wet kisses that ebbed and flowed in time with Morgan's thrusts along that spot inside him; in time with River's arches and upward rocking.

Morgan's nipples were hot, swollen when River finally let his fingers leave them. They'd probably be sore later, but that was good. Morgan would remember every time he moved, just like River would when he walked or sat or anything involving his ass, because Morgan wasn't slamming into him but there was an implacable slowness to the steady thrusts that was creating twinges, deep, hard twinges that River thought would ghost through him for days after.

"Gonna come, man," River moaned into Morgan's mouth, the words garbled but Morgan seemed to understand. "Gonna fucking come, Morgan. Right now, man..."

"Nnnngh." Not a word, not even recognisable, really, but the way Morgan was moving, a little bit harder, a little faster, seemed to be saying good, go for it, do it. And Morgan's cock, perfect damned beast that it was, was still right there, still sliding against River's feel-good spot, and River wasn't lying. He was coming.

He went tight, body arching harder, tighter under Morgan, around Morgan, rough spurts of seed painting his stomach, his chest. And Morgan hitched higher, teeth clenched, mouth too far away for kissing as River felt him swell, throb, grunt out a strangled sound that could have been anything at all. Heat filled him in swift, heavy pulses, and it was like nothing River had ever felt before. Shattering. Almost perfect, but for the fact that Simon wasn't there.

"He will be," Morgan whispered as he slowly collapsed onto River, still buried deep, still twitching just a little inside River's body. His voice sounded dry, sandpaper-rough, and River realised he'd said at least that last part out loud. "Soon, baby. All three of us. Soon."

Soon would have to do, River told himself, hands roaming slowly over Morgan's sweat-and-water-slick back. Finish the fucking Game and get back to HQ. Get Simon into bed with him and Morgan, all of them bare. Yeah, soon wasn't perfect, but River could deal.

He grinned against Morgan's neck, then licked slowly up to that square jaw. "Fucking awesome," River murmured, accepting Morgan's soft chuckle as his due. And "Stay," he added when Morgan would have moved, pulled out and away. "Just...stay." And Morgan did.

Chapter Eleven

Thank bloody Christ that Moon had hared off like she had some sort of bug up her bum as soon as the listening devices in the shower had picked up running water. The chit wasn't even slightly in the dark about what was going on and hadn't shown any sort of embarrassment over it, but yeah. Good that she hadn't wanted to hang about. Would have made it near impossible for Simon to do what he had to do, hearing his blokes going at it, bare as the day they were born.

He was still a little bit jealous, close to twenty-four hours later, but that wasn't surprising, Simon figured. He'd not been there, after all. Hadn't been able to feel River around him or even in him, naked and hot and... "And that's not helping, git," he muttered to himself, eyes closing for a minute to avoid Moon's sharp gaze. "Right, then." Louder, meant for his Gentlemen and Moon. "How's it looking, mates?"

"All clear on two," Hook answered, his voice sodding tinny through the ear bud's audio sensors, but then it always was. "No unusual activity. Man, there's this chick with tits like fucking watermelons."

"I saw her last night down here on one," Thorn answered, and that was the last thing Simon gave a toss about. "Kind of creepy, how they bounce around. Too much of a good thing. Moony's more my speed."

Moon snorted into the small microphone attached to her earpiece and rolled her eyes at Simon. "If you transfused your blood with NOX, you might be able to see my dust, Thorn. That's how out of your league I am. Okay. So nothing weird on one or two. River? What's going on up on three?"

Silence from River, and bloody fucking hell if Simon wasn't tense all of a sudden. More tense. Whatever the fuck.

"Riv's kinda busy, guys." Morgan. Thank bloody Christ. "He's telling some rent-boy about how mean I am. It's kind of cute, how he's glaring at me like I'm the biggest fucking prick in the world." Which did nothing to explain why Simon couldn't hear River. In fact...

"Get over there, love," Simon ordered quickly. "Don't have a signal on him. Like he's not even bloody there. Thought he was with you and overlapping."

"Fuck, how is that even possible?" Moon again and she looked just as freaked as Simon felt. "We had clear signal everywhere in the club before." The fact that they suddenly didn't have River was more than worrisome. It was impossible, or should have been.

Unless someone knew they were there and was blocking River's signal deliberately. Bloody fuck. Bloody fucking fuck. "Get our bloke and get the fuck out, love," Simon said, trying to stay calm, but it wasn't easy when he wanted to just get out of the hotel and to the damn club. Save his blokes and get the entire team the fuck out of Prague. "Now, Morgan."

Moon was waving, though. Her face looked tight, pinched, like she was just as worried as Simon. And she likely was, what with sharing the womb with River and all. "Morgan. Before you run in and maybe blow things, I need you to look around. You guys have been all over that club. Is there anything new that wasn't there last night? New tech or something. Look closely, okay? We're getting the rest of you just fine, so maybe there's a reason we've lost River now when we had him earlier."

Christ. Moon was right. No problems with River's signal until recently and he'd been coming in clear before. And that was exactly why he and Morgan never should have become invested in the bloke, Simon reminded himself. It clouded their judgement. Or it clouded Simon's, in any case, because Morgan hadn't sounded even slightly disturbed. Fuck.

"Fuck, you mean you guys can't hear him?" Morgan sounded sodding confused. "He's coming through to me just fine. Gin and tonic. Thanks." That last presumably to a bartender. "Man, he's making me sound like a total fucktard. If I didn't know better, I'd think he meant it."

"I've got him, too. Kid can spin a story." Hook, weighing in, and Simon let himself relax just a bit.

"Thorn? How about you?" Moon, sussing things out. Good girl.

"Nah. I've got Morgan and Hook, Moony, but nothing from baby bro."

Bloody hell, maybe he was getting too old for Games. Unless they involved people Simon didn't love, anyway. Shit. "Right. Seems something's limiting the distance on River's ear bud, then. Morgan, see if you can figure out what it is, yeah? Then get him away from it. Can't run the bloody Game if I don't know what the fuck's going on, can I?"

"I'm on it, Si. Whatever it is, you'll probably lose me for a minute, too. Hook can pass on what's happening if it takes longer than that. Cool?"

Not cool at all, Simon thought, even as his mouth said "Yeah, love. Know you've got it. Eyes open and whatnot."

Moon was giving him a sympathetic smile when Simon looked at her again, but her thumbs-up said good job just as loudly as words would have. The tightness around her eyes said she wasn't happy with the mystery dead zone around River, though. Dampening field, whatever it was. Bloody hell. They really needed to find out what was causing it. Find out, get a few of whatever it was shipped to one of the FGC's fronts, then to HQ. Get the tech teams on finding a way around it.

There was no reason to think it was anything more than just a random occurrence. Completely inconvenient when they were running a Game outside their usual type, but that sort of thing had been known to happen in the past. Not often, but it wasn't unheard of. And River was fine. Morgan had been looking right at him. It was just a tech glitch, something operating on a frequency that interfered with River's signal. That was all it could be. All it was.

Even so, Simon couldn't do anything but nod his agreement when Moon muttered "I don't like this," from just a few feet away. Yeah, he didn't like it either. Not a single bit. It was too...pat. Too convenient if the blighter they were after had any idea that he'd been targeted. Which he probably did, considering the

Russians had pulled back to let Simon's team make their Play.

"Hook, what's going on?" Moon demanded, her voice somehow harsh even though it was still measured, still calm. "Where are they?"

A moment, during which Simon figured Hook was asking just that on the secondary channel, then, "We have a problem, guys. I can hear them, but they can't hear me. The hustler River was talking to just said something about taking them up to the VIP level and it sounds like neither one of our guys can find a reason not to go." Hook paused and Simon could almost picture the frown that was likely on the Gentleman's face. "There's something wrong here, Simon. River's arguing in Czech."

Oh, fuck. That was more than just something wrong. River-as-whore didn't speak Czech. If the bloke was openly doing so, the Game was blown. Wide bloody open.

"Hook. Thorn. Get up there, both of you. Now!" Moon's words were snapped, the calm and cool tone completely gone. "Forget about the fucking target, get River and Morgan out! This Game is shot to hell!"

"You heard the Lady," Simon added, and yeah, he was snarling. Even as Moon started to break down their tech, Simon was snarling. "Extraction as we'd planned. Get your sodding asses in gear!"

The electronics broke down easily, modular as they were, and fit into the backpack Moon carried regularly. All but Simon's comm unit would be destroyed and discarded along the way to the rendezvous. And the bloody extraction team had better be ready, Simon thought with an internal growl.

More importantly, Thorn and Hook had better get Simon's blokes out of whatever was happening at the

Cern Oblocha Bar. He'd have their bollocks for earrings, otherwise.

"Right, then," Simon grunted, giving a last glance at the hotel room he and Moon had been using under cover of being a young married couple. Clothes still tossed carelessly over a chair, bed rumpled, toothbrushes visible through the bathroom door. "Off we go to tour the city at night. Obviously planning on coming back, aren't we?"

Moon nodded, a sweetly innocent smile lighting up her face. "I really want to go back to that bridge we saw this afternoon, honey," she chattered as they left the room, closing the door behind them. "That lady we met said it's so pretty at night when it's all lit up with fairy lights. At least, I think that's what she said. My German isn't that good, but..."

"It's better than mine," Simon answered, one arm around her shoulders as they waited for the elevator. "For all I know, she could have been saying there was a dog bathing in the public toilet."

The touristy banter took them from the hotel and down the street. Seemingly random turnings let them discard electronics and identification in rubbish bins and sewers, with a few pieces of the former dropped casually over the sides of the bridges that were so common.

It grated on Simon that he couldn't hear his team, but they couldn't take a chance on being caught with the kind of tech the FGC used. It wasn't so long since Prague had been under communist control; the local officials were still paranoid. One single ear bud would have him and Moon buried so deep, even the bloody Club might never get them out.

The rendezvous was smoky, filled with grizzled old men with cigars and pipes, the sweet stench of marijuana obvious under the more prevalent tobacco. Even so, Simon strolled lazily to the back, Moon right behind him, and when he gave the heavily bearded man behind the bar a nod and seemingly simple signal, a portion of the wall shifted, slid aside. It closed behind them with a soft hiss of air, leaving them in a surprisingly large room lit only by dim, flickering oil lamps.

"Nothing to do but wait," Moon said, and she was right, though she didn't sound pleased about it. Of course, neither was Simon.

* * * *

Morgan wasn't expecting the boot to his chest. Mostly because the little hustler River had been talking to just didn't look that flexible. Even so, the fucker had done it. Just looked at him after a few minutes of Morgan talking down to both him and River, saying Morgan doubted the guy could get them up to the next level; then the boy — because he looked like he was maybe seventeen — had taken a step back, and fuck if the little guy wasn't stronger than he looked, too. Not strong enough to put Morgan down, but he was off balance for a second from the impact.

A second too long, because River was suddenly standing in front of him, trying to protect him from a hooker, for fuck's sake, and…okay. Not good. Big guys, bigger than Morgan, and six of them. No fucking clue where they'd come from; they were just fucking there. Shit.

"No fight in club," one of them said, and Morgan wanted to say that he hadn't started it but the hustler was babbling a mile a minute and Morgan didn't speak Czech so he had no idea of what the kid was saying. It had the bruisers glaring at him, though, right up until River chimed in, looking frantic, all of a sudden.

More words and Morgan was still in the dark, but it was a cluster-fuck; it had to be. River wasn't supposed to speak Czech, or at least his cover didn't, but it for damned sure sounded like that was exactly what River was speaking and that meant...what? What the fuck was going on?

Simon would probably know, but Simon couldn't hear them, Morgan remembered. And they couldn't hear Simon, not with whatever it was that was dimming their transmissions.

"Look, guys," Morgan tried, "we'll just leave, okay? I'll take my fucking troublemaker and get out of your bar." He reached for River's shoulder, wanting to touch him, to at least try to get them out of what was a fucking mess, and the fist to his ear took him by surprise. So did the one to his spine. And one of the fucking thugs pushed River right into Morgan, River's body keeping Morgan from reacting, from hitting back, and that was it. That was all he knew, because another blow to the same ear had Morgan's head swimming, vision gone fuzzy, blurred.

He could hear River shouting something, but it was either in Czech again or Morgan's brain wasn't working right because he couldn't make any sense of the words. Someone was holding him up, though. Moving him, and he didn't think it was River. River wasn't that big, that rough. Fuck. It was all fucked up. Somehow they'd tipped their hand. Or else whoever was in charge wanted to sell River next.

Either way, Morgan needed to get it together. Needed to find a way to stop whatever was going on. River couldn't do it. He wasn't cut out for the sort of

Game they were running. Morgan didn't even know how he'd let Patrice make him think otherwise. Morgan had to fix things, or at least get River out...and he couldn't.

* * * *

Morgan thought he might have passed out, though he'd never done that before without having at least a few bullets in him. Still, swimming head and all, when Morgan's eyes finally cleared, when he could finally think again, he was lying on a couch, hands cuffed behind him, one of the thugs sitting on his legs and pointing a gun at him. Fuck. Fucking fuck.

"Riv," he tried to say but it came out as hiss when his jaw objected to moving. Even so, a shadow blocked the light above him and Morgan knew he was still having some weird sort of reaction to the head blows.

"People are not meat," the man standing there said, black brows drawn down over bright eyes. Rings through those eyebrows. More rings than Morgan could count running up the outside of the guy's ears. Rings in his nose, both nostrils and septum. Fuck, rings in the man's lips. Fucking insane. Distracting with the way they all moved. Morgan couldn't even focus on the guy's features. "I don't usually step in myself but you hit him last night. I can't overlook that. Not *him.*"

English. American English. And Morgan couldn't make any sense of it. Didn't much care to, either. "Get these fucking cuffs off me," he demanded and the guy snorted. Tossed his head, long black hair flying with the motion. "Where is he? Where's my fucking..."

"Whore?" A small, cold smile. "There are no whores here. And that one. The one you were with? He's not for you. You'll be released soon enough. My men will put you on a plane and you'll go back to wherever the fuck you came from. You won't come back to Prague and you definitely won't be abusing Ri...the guy you hit, ever again."

Oh. Oh, shit. It wasn't about the Game, it was about River. The fucker really did want to sell Morgan's lover. Sell him to some fucking bastard who'd ruin River, then kill him. Jesus fucking Christ, how was that any better than leaving River with Morgan, even with the shithead thinking River was being beaten?

"Fuck you." His jaw still objected to speaking, but fuck it. "What the fuck did you do to him? River would never leave me! If you hurt him, I'll rip your fucking head off, you piece of shit!" He bucked, ignoring the gun pointed at him, ignoring the fact that his own actions could make it go off. "Run, River! If you can hear me, run!"

A sigh from the bastard, then the gleams of silver were gone, turned away. "Subdue him, please."

"Fuck you!" Morgan managed before everything went black.

* * * *

God, what the hell had just happened? First the rent-boy he'd been talking to had got all...River didn't know what, really. Offended, maybe, when River didn't leap at the chance to be 'rescued' from Morgan. Then that same young hustler had gone nuts at Morgan disbelieving that anyone so cheap and tawdry looking could get River and Morgan to the VIP level. It had been a good call, though, because River hadn't believed it either. The boy honestly hadn't looked that special, right up until he'd kicked Morgan in the head.

River had a vague recollection of screaming in Czech, trying to make the boy and the thugs who'd appeared then understand that Morgan wasn't actually a danger, but that had failed. One of the thugs had taken Morgan down while the other had somehow managed to drag River off to wherever the hell he was right then. There had been a hallway. River remembered that much.

What he didn't recall was seeing where the first thug had taken Morgan, damn it, and that was the important thing. Almost as important was the question of why River was being held prisoner when he hadn't thrown so much as a single punch, but there was no question about his captive state. River had tried the door. He'd even tried picking the lock but whoever had set things up in the stupid club clearly knew what they were doing. River couldn't manage to escape without the sort of tools he didn't have.

The only hopeful thought he could come up with was that Simon and Moon would know he and Morgan were in trouble. Hook and Thorn were on the premises and would find them. Assuming that Morgan hadn't been taken somewhere else, but River doubted that.

It was too easy to keep them both in the club for whatever it was the current proprietor, who River guessed was the one who'd had him and Morgan ambushed, had in mind.

Either way, the team would rescue them. River knew it. Had to believe it. He didn't like that he and Morgan had been separated, but Morgan was fine. Morgan had to be fine. "I can't lose him. I just can't," River whispered to himself, but also to Simon, wherever he was. Simon might not be answering on the ear bud, but River needed him to know that Morgan was just as important to him as to Simon. "I can't lose either of you."

"Much concern for abusing bastard." The voice wasn't familiar and came from somewhere near the ceiling. "Not smart, pretty boy."

River would never admit that he jumped at hearing the unexpected words. When he did his debrief, he would present himself as having been calm and cool when that voice sounded. That future fiction didn't change the fact that he did jump, though. Jumped so much that he almost fell off the sofa he'd sat down on after the first five minutes or so of his captivity.

The voice was heavily accented; the words, in English, sounded unwieldy.

"You don't get to call me pretty," he responded in Czech. It was close enough to Russian that he hadn't had much trouble learning the nuances on the flight over. "Where is my friend, you thick-necked piece of shit?" Maybe being confrontational was the wrong way to go, but fuck it. He needed to know where Morgan was. Needed to know he was all right.

"But you are pretty," the voice replied in the same language, sounding less thug-like in what River presumed to be the speaker's native tongue. "A very pretty boy. Far too pretty to allow a beast such as your former friend to treat you that way."

Oh, shit. That didn't sound good. Nor did the constant 'pretty', now that River was thinking about it. Simon and Morgan had suspected human trafficking in the club. What if this was how they got their...merchandise?

"We had a misunderstanding," River said bluntly, shoving the fear and anger down as far as he could manage. "It was a slap; nothing more! Let me out of here! And I want to see Mor...my friend! Now, damn it!"

A chuckle came through the system, loud and clear, and it was only then that River realised he couldn't hear the music from the club. The room he was in was soundproofed. Shit, that probably meant the team couldn't hear what was going on, which made sense since he was getting nothing through his ear bud. It wasn't the kind of sense River wanted things to make, but there it was.

"You are even prettier when you're angry, pretty boy, but you're in no position to make demands. My employer will speak with you soon. It would be wise to have a less commanding attitude when he does."

Shit-shit-shit-shit-*fuck*! He was going to be sold off to some perverted fucker who liked to own people! And God knew what had happened to Morgan. Hell, considering how alpha-male Morgan got when confronted, there was a good chance that Morgan was...

No. River swallowed hard, keeping tears from his eyes by sheer force of will. *Morgan's not dead. He can't be. Simon will kill him if he's let himself get dead. And probably kill me, too.*

River looked around the room again, still seeing the same shit he'd noticed when he'd first been abandoned there. The sofa he was sitting on, a chair...a narrow table against one wall that held three crystal or maybe just cut glass decanters, along with two glasses.

There was nothing that would help him escape. Or not until someone came for him, River realised. One of the decanters would work nicely as a weapon if River broke it off below the neck.

It would take very careful timing and he had to hope that, whoever the 'employer' was, they'd show up before River was too exhausted to do anything but fall over in an adrenaline-crashed and sleep-deprived faint, but it was his only option. As such, he had to take it.

He pushed up from the sofa and crossed the room, lifting each of the decanters and pulling out the stoppers, as though he was smelling the liquids inside. He was really assessing the weight and quality of each, though, trying to determine which would make the best weapon.

He'd decided on the decanter that held what smelt like Brandy when he heard the small *snick* of the door's lock disengaging, but he pretended he hadn't noticed. In fact, he picked up one of the glasses and wrapped the fingers of his other hand around the neck of the chosen decanter, listening for the sound of the door closing. Once it did, he waited a few more seconds, hoping the intruder would come closer as he lifted the decanter, preparing to shatter it against the edge of the table.

"I'd really rather you didn't." This voice was different. American, rather than Czech. And it hit River hard, right in his gut, because he knew it. Knew it well enough that it froze him right where he was. "Those decanters are antiques and bordering on priceless. If you really want to fight with me, we can always go hand to hand. Again. Who knows? You might do better this time. Or not." A laugh River also knew well. "Probably not, if I'm being honest."

"You bastard," River said quietly, setting the decanter down with care. "You fucking *bastard*! I thought you were *dead*!" He spun quickly, hurling the glass he still held, sending it flying unerringly and with force.

One black-clad arm rose, intercepting the missile, and the man facing him didn't even flinch when the glass shattered, a few shards scoring small wounds on the nearer cheek.

"No, you didn't," the man said, and while the black hair and piercings were unexpected, the rest wasn't. "You never thought I was dead; not even for a second. You're just pissed off that I got the drop on you. And you know what? Fair enough. *I'm* pissed off that whatever the fuck happened after I left has you winding up in Prague looking like a whore and letting some fucking shithead beat on you, so I guess we're even. That glass you threw, by the way? That was your one free shot. Count yourself lucky that I even gave you *one* because I really do want to beat the shit out of you for taking up with that loser."

There were so many things wrong with what was happening that River couldn't even begin to list them; not even to himself. It didn't matter, though. What mattered was, "Morgan. Where is he? I need to see him."

Bright blue eyes rolled under black-as-night brows. "Not gonna happen. I've seen to it. Now, are you planning on telling me how the fuck you ended up falling so far in the last few years? Because that's the part I'm still not getting, River. Shit, you were always the smart one. How did you end up as some fucking asshole's boy-toy?"

Something inside River tightened. Clenched. Made him feel sick, all of a sudden. "What do you mean, you've 'seen to it'? Seen to what?" God, if Morgan was hurt or worse, River would never forgive himself. He felt like he was going to puke, all of a sudden.

Some of that must have shown on his face because a look of disgust passed over the black-haired man's face. "Relax. It's nothing permanent. I don't need an international incident making things worse. My people are making sure he wakes up somewhere safe, with a ticket for a flight back to the U.S. that leaves in the morning. The rest of my people will make sure he can't get a plane back to Prague for the next five years or so, and by then he will have found some other pretty boy to abuse. You don't need to worry about him any more, okay?"

River turned his sickened gaze into a glare. "I'll always worry about him. I love him. And he barely touched me last night. It wasn't... Fuck. I can't tell you." Because he'd just then realised that the guy he was talking to was the 'employer' the disembodied voice had referred to. He didn't want to believe it, but who else would have come to him when that voice had said the 'employer', which River took to mean 'boss', was coming for him?

That seemed to give the black-haired, pierced man pause. "I thought you could tell me anything," he said, sounding a little sad. River knew it was sadness. Even if they hadn't seen each other in years, he still recognised the tone. "I know we've been out of touch for a while, but I really thought you would still trust me, River. Even with a few years of silence between us."

"You thought wrong." God, it fucking hurt to say that, but, considering what River finally knew about the boss-man and the human trafficking and the dead young people, he couldn't afford to be sentimental. "And it hasn't been 'a few years', it's been *six*, you jackass. How can you do it? How can you be selling people and letting them die?" It wasn't his brightest moment ever, to be asking that, but he needed to know. "Tell me! How can you be doing things that are even worse than the Russian Mob you took over from? God! Before you go preaching to me about Morgan and one slap-for-show, maybe you should think about all the kids you've sold into slavery!"

The man literally swayed. River saw him do it. "I. What? What the fuck are you talking about? I don't... And what do you know about the Russian Mob? I mean, okay. I took this place over from them, even ran them out, but...*they're* the ones who were selling...you know what? Never mind. Who are you working for, River? Give me a name."

River shrugged, and, while he wasn't entirely sure he believed the so-familiar but so clearly unknown man, he answered. "Let's say that Moon and I are following a family tradition and leave it at that."

It obviously took the guy a moment to process that, but then he burst into motion. "We really need to let my people know that your 'friend' isn't one of the bad guys. Sooner would be better than later. They weren't told to take any special care with him. Come on."

River couldn't argue with that. Wouldn't have, even if he'd had the breath. He didn't, though. He was running after the guy he'd never expected to see again, much less in Prague, too hard to argue; especially when he was in complete agreement.

Chapter Twelve

The Cern Oblacha Bar appeared stunningly normal when Simon looked at it from across the way. In fact, it didn't look like anything out of the ordinary had happened there at all that night. No police cars, no surprising numbers of thug-like blokes wandering about outside.

On the one hand, that was a good thing. It implied that his people had possibly made it out. On the other hand...it could also mean that they hadn't. That Simon's entire team had been subdued without anyone noticing.

Either one was possible, really. Based upon the intel, whoever had taken over the club might actually be good enough to manage that.

"We shouldn't be here," Moon murmured, and the local operative they'd followed there from the dingy backroom of the tavern agreed with a grunt. The man wasn't a Gentleman by any stretch of the imagination, but he was on the FGC's payroll, and as such Simon trusted him almost as far as he could throw him. "We're supposed to be at the rendezvous."

Simon couldn't say she was wrong, but sod it. His blokes were inside the fucking bar, the last he knew. He couldn't just run back to the meeting point without seeing whether there was anything unusual going on, except there truly didn't seem to be. "Ring them," he ordered, still staring at the building.

"Simon," Moon said, clearly building up to something, but Simon wasn't in the mood to hear it. He was tense. Bloody fuck, tense had come and gone. He was whatever someone would be when the two people he cared most about in the world were unaccounted for, and that was far beyond just *tense*.

"Do it. Ring them. We can ditch your phone after but I need to know. Try Hook and Thorn first." It hurt like a punch to the gut to say that, but Hook and Thorn were the ones they'd heard from last. "They might know something. If not, try Morgan and Riv. I need to know whether we're leaving my... Bloody fucking Christ. Just do it, Moon!"

He counted it as a win when she pulled her FGC-issue phone from her pants pocket. He counted it as a sign of her concern that she didn't ask him to make it an official order. Then again, one of the Gentlemen in danger was her twin brother.

"Hook and Thorn are out," Moon muttered after a few seconds of whispers. "They're halfway to the rendezvous, but neither of them has seen River or Morgan. Hook thinks they might have been taken inside the club."

That wasn't at all what Simon had wanted to hear, but he kept his eyes locked on the stone building and nodded slowly. "Right, then. Get out of here. Piotr's our local contact, so he knows all the alleys and such.

He'll be sure to get you to the rendezvous, if he wants to get paid. Lie low for a while. If I'm not there in three hours, you're in charge. Get yourself and the rest of the team back home, yeah?"

Moon glared at him. Simon could see it from the corner of his eye, though he didn't bother to turn his full gaze on her. "No," she said bluntly. "Are you out of your fucking mind? I know you think you're bulletproof or whatever, but you're one man, Simon. There's no way I'm leaving you here to run whatever stupid-ass kamikaze *Game* you've suddenly come up with! Dude! That's just not cool!"

Christ, she sounded just like her brother. So much so that Simon felt his heart being squeezed in his chest. Not literally, of course. It was sheer emotion creating the sensation, but that didn't stop it from seeming completely real.

"Don't expect you to understand it," Simon grated out as quietly as he could. "Don't even expect you to be happy about it. It's still a sodding order, you bint, so get your ass moving. Or do I need to knock you the out and have Piotr carry you? Because I can and I will, as you well know."

It wasn't a threat but a simple statement of fact, that last, and Moon really did know it. They'd sparred more than a few times back at HQ and, while Moon was very, very good, Simon knew he was better. So did Moon, though she seemed reluctant to admit it just then.

"Fine. I'll go." It was an easier surrender than he'd been expecting. "But if you're not there in *two hours* we're coming back here to find out why not. I'll worry about censure when we're back home."

Well, there wasn't really much he could do about it once she'd headed off to meet the rest of the team, was there? "Fine," Simon grunted. "Now go."

She finally did, taking Piotr with her, and Simon figured Christ must be getting tired of all the thanks being sent his way, but fuck it. All he could do was hope the bloke kept listening because there wasn't a single chance that Simon would be leaving before he found his men and got them both the fuck out of the bloody club. Assuming they were still there, which was actually a rather dubious proposition. What were the chances that Morgan and River would still be inside after however long it had been since Simon had lost contact and called the Game Over?

He circled around the building as casually as possible, only hoping he didn't look keyed up. It was when he reached the back of the club and paused to take a few long, slow breaths in the shadows that Simon finally relaxed just a little. Then the steel door in the long brick and stone wall of the building opened and he froze, trying to stay out of the extended rectangle of light.

"I don't know why they're not answering, but I know their route."

For a moment, Simon thought it was River speaking and he couldn't make sense of the words in conjunction with their meaning. Then "Jesus, man, what the fuck?" *That* was River. Simon figured he'd been fooled by hearing another person with an American accent.

Many people in Prague spoke English, but Americans weren't entirely common; at least not at places like the Cern Oblacha Bar.

"Calm down," the first voice said. "I told you, I know their route. They're only twenty minutes ahead of us and we're not lugging a couple hundred pounds of meat. We'll catch up."

"He's not *meat*." River again. "He's my...fuck if I know what he is, dude, but he's my something. You better hope your fucktards haven't hurt him or we're gonna have some fucking problems!"

The voices were growing quieter as they moved away, and Simon breathed a sigh of relief when the open door finally finished its overly-slow slide to closed. He was also slightly relieved at the implication that Morgan was still alive somewhere, but the sheer degree of concern in the unknown voice worried him. Not that he would be anything but worried until Morgan was in front of him, safe and as unharmed as possible.

He followed as closely as he could without looking like he was trailing River and...some pillock with black hair that was just as long as River's blond. It was bizarre, Simon noticed vaguely. Similar heights, though the black-haired berk was an inch or so taller. Similar builds. The two men even moved in a like-enough fashion, but maybe the black-haired bastard was mirroring River, trying to make it seem like they had something in common.

He considered announcing his presence, seeing as River and the git appeared to be on speaking terms, but that would be foolish. The black-haired prick might be leading River into a trap that couldn't be traced to the club, after all. Not that Simon believed River would be foolish enough to trust some random bloke, but, whatever the case, Morgan was already in dubious circumstances and Simon couldn't help that at the moment. The least he could do was act as backup for his other bloke, if it became necessary.

He almost stumbled when the black-haired git stopped suddenly, but no one who mattered was looking. River had actually tripped a bit, and the black-haired prat was steadying him. Then the unfamiliar man spoke in Czech, apparently to the two bruisers who'd stopped when River and the git did.

Simon wasn't close enough to hear much, but he thought River mentioned a man; likely Morgan.

One of the big, burly bastards stepped closer and shrugged. "Taken care of." That much Simon heard without any doubt.

"Where. Is. He." River again, sounding so blunt and tight that Simon knew he was about to go on the offensive. "The dark-haired man who was with me before."

The spokesman for the two thugs laughed and said something in a language Simon didn't know, obviously as an aside to his cohort, and the black-haired pillock answered in that same language, sounding more than irritated, which had Simon reaching a level of anxiety he hadn't expected after the slight belief from earlier that Morgan was okay.

That anxiety only increased when the black-haired shit calmly pulled a gun from somewhere and shot the main thug in the shoulder. Simon didn't need to understand the language the black-haired man was speaking to understand, "Show me or you're next." And maybe the bloke with the black hair wasn't actually a git or a pillock or even a bloody berk because the speed he prodded the remaining thug to use was inspiring.

Simon took off after River and the black-haired stranger, and when the uninjured thug stopped in the middle of one of Prague's many bridges, babbling in that same unknown language and pointing, Simon took a leap of faith.

A leap of faith and a leap of body, really, because he didn't stop when the thug did. Didn't even pause to wonder whether he'd made the right assumption based upon the gestures. He just ran towards the trio of River, thug, and black-haired man, and leapt up onto the stone railing of the bridge.

He managed to look over his shoulder as he dove into the water, giving an obviously surprised River a nod. Then he was airborne for a single suspended second and the wet cold closed around him, but that didn't matter. He'd heard enough of what River and the unexpected ally had said to know that Morgan had been knocked out and an unconscious body would move with the current but not in the way that someone awake and aware would.

He would catch up to Morgan. Simon was sure of that much. He would catch up and he would pull his love from the icy water, and…well, then he'd go back and get River out of whatever Riv had got into. After that, they'd get the hell out of Prague and the Russian fucking Mafia could try again with some other team.

"-imon!" he heard when his head broke up from the dive. "What the fuck are you doing! Do you have any idea how dirty that water is? Get out of there, for fuck's sake!"

It was only then that Simon considered the thug's gesture might have been towards something other than the water. *Bloody hell.*

* * * *

It was the sudden shock of cold water that roused Morgan from his stupor.

Oh, he had a vague recollection of being hit and cuffed. His wrists still ached a little, even with the sheer chill of the water he felt on his face. There was a hazy notion that he'd lost...something. Something important.

He was so tired, though. So fucking tired. Probably from getting the shit kicked out of him because that was never a relaxing and revitalising experience. And yet, the thought plagued him. He was missing...something.

It came back to him slowly, more slowly than he wanted, really, but he probably couldn't have handled it if the memory had come any faster.

River.

Morgan being taken out by a boy who couldn't have been more than seventeen, for fuck's sake, and that was beyond embarrassing.

There had been some pierced guy with black hair.

Another blow to the head. Maybe a taser, too, because he had that daggy feeling, like every cell in his body had fired too often in too short a time.

River. He had to save River.

The yawning chasm of unconsciousness beckoned, even with the cold water Morgan still felt soaking his face and hair, but it wasn't appealing enough for him to forget the situation. River was in trouble and there had been some sort of communication problems earlier, and that meant Morgan was River's only chance unless Hook and Thorn had been able to work an extraction, which wasn't likely.

Then again, Morgan realised, holding himself still just in case, he and River had been separated back at the club. There was a possibility that the rest of the on-site team had been able to extract River but not *him*.

Oddly enough, Morgan was fine with that idea. Simon had been off-site, so Simon was fine, and that had something in Morgan's gut relaxing. That River might possibly be safe as well only added to that sensation.

If I don't make it, they'll have each other. Neither of them will be left alone.

Okay, it was a slightly disturbing thought, but it actually helped. And Simon would look after Rico. Morgan didn't doubt that for a moment. Simon loved the little girl almost as much as Morgan did, though at twelve years old, and considering Rico's upbringing and special skills, the girl wasn't as childlike as Morgan assumed most girls her age would be, out in the real world.

Still, Simon would look after her if Morgan didn't make it, and that was a comforting thought. River and Rico seemed to get along too, which was still more of a good thing. When Simon and River became a couple, Rico would have two parents again.

Morgan frowned on the inside, though he didn't actually let his face reflect it. When had he decided that he wasn't going to make it? He was still alive, damn it, and he'd be getting out of whatever the fuck he'd got himself into. It might take some doing, but he would.

He would get free and find out whether River was safe or not. Then he'd either admit that the fucking Game had gone completely *tits-up*, as Simon would say, or he'd find out everyone was still in Play.

He was unarmed, of course, but that didn't mean he was helpless. Far from it. After as many sessions as he'd been through with Tink, Morgan was fairly sure that he was just as dangerous without weapons as with them. And he had the advantage. Whoever was holding him and apparently trying to rouse him with ice water to the face... Clearly they thought he was just what he'd pretended to be at the club. A closeted, abusive shit who'd had to take his boy-toy to another country in order to feel safe.

Morgan didn't speak Czech. He'd counted on his ear bud and River or Simon to translate for him. He still recognised disdain when he heard it from the person he'd already known was in the room with him. He hadn't been aware of a second person being there, but there was a second voice, too.

Then another dousing of ice-cold water hit his face and he forced himself to respond sluggishly.

"Wha...what the fuck?" Good. He sounded groggy, even to himself. His eyes opened, blinking away the liquid that had gathered in his lashes, and even though the room he saw wasn't well lit, he knew immediately that he wasn't at the Cern Oblacha Bar any more. He could make out rough stone in the walls, and while the club wasn't a new structure, it wasn't old enough for that. "Where am I? What's going on?"

"Told to send you back to America on plane." The one who spoke was an old man. He had to be at least seventy unless he'd led a truly hard life. "Given much cash money to do so."

Well, that was hopeful, sort of. Assuming the team had extracted River, Morgan could live with flying back to the U.S. with his tail between his legs.

The other man, who was much younger, said something in what Morgan thought was Czech, and the old man laughed. There was something in that laugh that Morgan didn't trust, though. Something in the younger man's gaze that only reinforced that feeling.

"*Much* cash money," the older man repeated. "But is more if no plane. No return to America. You go with grandson. No blood in home."

Seriously? These two guys thought Morgan was going to just go along with them so he could apparently be killed somewhere else? Really?

"Can't move," Morgan muttered, forcing himself to sound spacey, and, while it was a bit of a lie, it wasn't far from the truth. His whole body still hurt. Even so, he was pretty sure he could take out both men. Neither of them seemed to be terribly fit. "And my passport's at my hotel. Can't fly anywhere without it…"

He pretended to nod off, all the while plotting the demise of the old man and the younger one. He would need to be fast. The old guy first because he seemed to be in charge, then the young one. The young one was in better shape but didn't seem too swift, Morgan decided, watching both men through barely slitted eyes.

He would gather himself, and when they were least expecting it Morgan would spring into action. It might not be PC, but fuck if he cared. He was absolutely willing to kill some old guy and the old guy's grandson, seeing as they were actively planning his own death. For something as paltry as money.

Fuck them. Morgan had a family to get back to and he was ready, willing and able to do whatever it took to accomplish that.

It was a far better reason for killing than money would ever be.

Unfortunately, Morgan never had a chance to put the plan he was developing into action because, the next thing he knew, there were more people in the room and then the yelling began.

The yelling turned into screaming within seconds. Morgan's captors were apparently more than unhappy about something, but fuck it if Morgan cared because the answering voices, the ones shouting back, though less loudly... Oh, he'd know Simon and River anywhere. And as he did know them as well as he did, Morgan also knew he needed to move. Quickly.

He rolled across the old, uneven stones he hadn't noticed he was lying on, one hand sliding out to grab the younger of his captors by the ankle. Then he dragged the fucker down, throwing him off balance and against the older man—the first one's grandfather, it seemed.

A flailing foot whacked him in the head, but Morgan held on, seeing stars rather than the small, dimly lit, dingy room that smelt of mildew, and fought against the hands that were trying to make him release the asshole he was holding on to for dear life...maybe literally.

"Dude." The hands on him softened and Morgan shook his head as the stars faded a bit. "Dude," again, and Morgan let his grip on the shit relax when he realised it was River's hands he was feeling on his own. "Morgan, man. It's okay. You can let that ugly fucker go now. Sky has him."

A snort sounded then and Morgan knew that particular sound so well he couldn't help laughing, the amusement feeling rusty with disuse for a moment. "Might be more accurate to say the piss-ant git's pet thugs have him, but either way, love... Not quite thrilled to see you holding on to some strange bloke so tightly. Or are you trying to make me jealous?"

The stars faded more, until Morgan could actually see Simon. He couldn't help the grin that curved his lips. "Si? Is there some reason you look like a drowned rat?" He finally let go of the ankle he'd been holding and slowly sat up to take inventory.

Simon, check. Definitely looking just like Morgan had said, and smelling a bit like a drowned rat, too, but still pretty much the best thing Morgan had ever seen.

River, check. Very much *not* dead and apparently not in the sort of trouble Morgan had feared. River was dry and still in the club clothes from earlier, which didn't seem to bode well for their Game, but fuck it. Better a live River and Simon than any degree of successful, as far as Morgan was concerned right then.

"You're okay," Morgan said softly, not at all surprised when some previously unrecognised tightness in his gut eased. "Thank fuck."

"You can thank fuck later, love," Simon said, snarky as usual, and that was just another sign that whatever was happening with the Game, Simon and River were fine. "Right now, you should probably be thanking this tosser."

Morgan frowned slightly and followed the direction of Simon's sharp head-jerk. His heart almost burst with trying to speed up too fast when it had finally been slowing. "That's the piece of shit who—"

"Who bought our act so much he couldn't let you hit me again!" River sounded almost panicked, which was strange enough to have Morgan dragging his eyes from the pin-cushion-faced guy with the black hair. "He wouldn't have done any of it if he'd known it was all an act. Swear, man."

It wasn't anything Morgan wanted to believe, but River looked so damned sincere, he just couldn't bring himself to doubt those words. He was still possibly concussed, though, so Morgan wasn't sure he'd actually understood.

"Um, could someone explain this to me in very small words? Seriously, guys. My head is killing me right now from Tweedle-Dum's boot...and possibly whatever the fuck Mr Nice-Guy over there did to me." Morgan slowly forced himself to sit up, trying not to groan at the pain in his jaw, where the hustler had kicked him, along with the rest of his upper body. "And if someone could give me a hand up, that would be good, too. This floor is hard and fucking cold."

Chapter Thirteen

River could feel himself blushing, but he'd been doing that on a fairly regular basis lately. While this particular blush could be traced directly to his own embarrassment and shame at having lied to Simon and Morgan, he was still almost used to the sensation of a hot face that was undoubtedly bright pink.

"Okay." Morgan sounded just as stunned as he looked, though River didn't think it was from the blows to the head, or not entirely. "*He*," Morgan pointed at Sky. "I don't even know how to say it."

River didn't even need to look at Simon to know that the still-damp and now slightly shivering Englishman was rolling his eyes.

"The bloke with all the pricks in his face is our target," Simon said bluntly, boiling down what River had already said into something so compact River couldn't help but be envious. "For whatever reason and by some undoubtedly nefarious method, he and his lot ousted the Russians from the club. Seems he was trying to return some of the young ones with second thoughts to their families, or at least to somewhere a whole hell of a lot better for them than bloody Prague. Turns out some of his 'helpers'," Simon sneered the word, "were taking advantage by killing some and selling others off, while pocketing the funds meant for relocation. Seems they were doing the same to some of the Russians, as well."

River almost laughed, but he couldn't quite manage it. Not when he still felt so off-kilter.

"Oh, yeah," Simon added, "and this bloke. Sky. He's our Riv's *other* twin. Be a right shame to turn him over to the Russians now, considering."

Sky laughed, though it sounded more like a sharp bark to River, and that couldn't be good. Then Sky spoke and River knew he was right.

"Yeah. About that." Sky sounded pissed off. Not to anyone else, River was sure, but River knew. "Seeing as I've been fighting the good fight, as *Angel* once said—or as Angel said more fucking times than I can count—and you people are the reason I'm out of my safety zone, *and* I saved your fucking life...Morgan, right?"

River saw Morgan nod from the corner of his eye. As much as he was worried about Morgan, River knew better than to take his eyes off Sky. 'Other twin' or not, Sky was fucking dangerous.

"Morgan, then." Sky nodded, his tone merely conversational unless someone knew what to look for. "I left the club. You think nobody knows that by now? The fucking Russians—by which I mean the organised crime portions of the Russians, not the rest of them— probably have half their local contingent sweeping the streets for me already. They might not have seen me go, but they know what I look like and they'll know I'm out with nothing but two half-wit guards and some hustler. There's about a zero chance of me getting back inside. So thanks for that, assholes. The least you can do is get me the fuck out of the Czech Republic."

Oh, Lord. That was Sky all over. Yeah, his brother was pissed definitely off. River couldn't even claim that Sky didn't have good reason to be. Whatever Sky had really been up to, River and the FGC had fucked it up so far that 'fucked up' was at least three planets away. And Sky really had saved Morgan, though Morgan wouldn't have been in that sort of danger if Sky hadn't put him there, however unknowingly.

"Whatever," Morgan said, waving the hand River wasn't currently holding. "I'm still… Sorry, maybe I got hit in the head harder than I thought, but I thought Moony was Riv's twin. Isn't she? I don't get it."

River felt his own eyes rolling when Simon snorted for what seemed like the twentieth time in ten minutes.

"Honestly, love?" Simon looked just as amusedly baffled as he sounded. "All you've just heard and the only thing you're wondering about is that? Bloody hell. We need to get to the rendezvous. You clearly need medical attention."

Even as Sky ordered his one remaining thug to 'clean up this mess and disappear them and yourself' with a nod in the direction of the two men who'd been planning to kill Morgan, River wasn't sure that it was anything close to a good idea to take Sky back to the U.S., but it wasn't up to him. It was up to Simon, thank God, as team handler.

"If we're going to run around Prague to the rendezvous," River finally chimed in, "Sky needs to look like…someone who's not Sky."

"And quickly," Simon agreed, clearly checking his watch. "Have a feeling the rest of the team's going to be looking for us at that Cern Oblacha Bar if we're not where we need to be in…bloody fuck. Forty minutes, mates."

Morgan squeezed, tightening his fingers around River's and River turned his attention back to his wounded…whatever the fuck Morgan was to him. It was the same thing *Simon* was to him, but Simon was damp, not damaged.

"We should hurry," Morgan said simply. Then not so simply, "Sky, before your thug shoots the guys who were about to kill me, we need their clothes. Not the thug's. The other two. Riv, I hate to say this, but you need to switch pants with your brother. Simon, pull the old guy's pants on over your wet ones and take the younger asshole's shirt. Thugly's going to have to trade shirts with me, just in case someone noticed me being hauled out of the club and happened to be paying attention. Get started. We have five minutes…seven, tops. Move!"

River blinked and saw Sky do so, too, but Simon simply started following Morgan's orders. "Um, Simon?" River tried, and Simon smirked.

"What can I say? Our bloke's fucking amazing under pressure, yeah? Remind me to tell you the *real* story of how we met. Later."

River tried to laugh, but he couldn't. He was having too much trouble trying to peel the shiny black pants from his body while attempting to will the erection he'd suddenly sprung at knowing Morgan could be so masterful, even while injured. It wasn't in any way easy, or less than embarrassing. Especially in front of his own brother.

* * * *

Bloody hell, what a cluster-fuck. Simon honestly couldn't recall even hearing about a Game that had gone so wrong.

Morgan could have died. River could have been separated from them forever. Moon, Thorn and Hook could have—would have—died if Morgan's plan hadn't worked out, and their target had turned out to be River and Moon's brother, of all sodding things!

Add in the decidedly unpleasant bacteria that had managed to become lodged in Simon's lungs and intestines from his completely unnecessary swim in the Vltava, or whatever they called the branch of the river in Prague that Simon had dived into, and *cluster-fuck* was actually an understatement.

It didn't help that Hook and Thorn had been completely caught up in keeping Moon and Sky from killing each other, possibly literally, for the entire flight back, either. Simon didn't actually remember all of that, but the first few hours had been impressive. Then the fever had really started to take hold and Simon's ability to remain coherent and conscious had slipped. It also didn't help that no one had any idea about where Sky had disappeared to once the plane set down, but Simon couldn't worry too much about it right then.

He'd been sicker than sick at the time. So sick that the rest of the team had been debriefed without him in the six days since they'd made it back to HQ. So sick that Doc had slipped Simon into what Jericho called 'the big tub of purple goo'. It was actually Banta Gel, something Doc had come up with a while earlier. Simon didn't know how it worked, but it sped healing and helped kill off the germs Jericho called 'evil'.

It wasn't the first time Simon had been slimed, actually, but the last had involved physical injuries rather than bugs or whatever. At least the goo seemed to work faster on germs. Simon had only needed to spend half an hour in the tank before being hauled out for the rest of his recovery.

Doc Pritchard thought the illness had hit so hard and so fast owing to a combination of adrenaline and the fact that Simon had never been to the Czech Republic before. While the entire team had been vaccinated before the trip and no one else had become ill, it seemed Simon was more sensitive to the ever-changing contaminants in the river water. Lucky him.

Actually, very lucky him, because unless something truly bizarre showed up in his blood work all of a sudden, Simon was going to be released from the Med Centre later that day.

"Hi, Simon!"

Simon laughed as Jericho came barrelling into his room. "Princess! You're looking...guilty, if I'm taking a guess. Now, what on earth have you been up to, hmmm?" He arched a brow as the girl jumped up to sit on the edge of his hospital bed. "Must be a real big bit of badness to have you looking so contrite." He grinned smugly, teasing.

Jericho might be a forty-year-old trapped in a twelve-year-old body sometimes, and the girl might know things nobody should ever know ahead of time, but she was still Simon's Princess, his Petal. The daughter he'd never expected to have. To be fair, Morgan had never expected to have a child either, and as Simon considered himself and Morgan — and now River — to be a permanent thing, Petal belonged to all of them. Fortunately, Jericho being who and what Jericho was, Simon was sure she already knew all that.

Just as he was certain she knew Simon could always tell when she was feeling guilty and apologetic. Like she was right then.

"Well?"

"I didn't do anything!"

Simon snorted softly. "Wasn't born yesterday, as you well know," he murmured, lifting one hand to grip the much smaller hand Jericho was holding out towards him. "And I know I'm 'old' and whatnot now, but I remember very clearly that when I was your age? 'I didn't do anything' meant I'd bloody well done *something*. Out with it, Petal. You'll feel better once you share, yeah?"

Jericho resisted for a bit longer, but she finally came clean and, while Simon wasn't sure how he felt about what she'd said, he didn't see the harm in it. That didn't mean he was necessarily going to keep it to himself, though.

"I know," Jericho said, sighing softly. Simon hadn't even answered her confession yet, but he was used to the girl knowing things without hearing them. "I know you're gonna tell Morgan and Riv. I want you to." Her eyes went slightly far-away and her voice didn't deepen but it became more remote. "There's a reason for everything. This has to happen. If not now, then years from now, but now would be better for all of us."

It still creeped him out a fair bit when Jericho went all psychic-friends-without-the-network, but Simon figured she knew as much.

"Right, then. I'll mention it to my blo…to Morgan, Princess. Not right away, but soon."

Just like that the girl went from creepy-strange to normal-enough. All it took was focusing eyes and a big, toothy smile. "Thanks, Simon! And Marcus says the rooms next to ours are gonna be vacant in a few days! Shariann's moving in with Tina, so if River wanted to move closer, he could, and I looked at the designs from when they first built HQ and...it's not a bearing wall. Just so's you know."

Jericho grinned again then hopped off the edge of the bed. "I really want to spend tonight up at the Ranch. I mean, I know it's your first night out of Med Centre, but one of the horses is gonna have her baby tonight and I figure there's gonna be enough 'Simon's first night out of Med' in the next twenty years 'cause you're reckless and stuff, but how often can I see a baby horse being born? You don't mind, right? Morgan said it's okay, but I want to make sure you know it doesn't mean I don't love you if I'm way up there on the Ranch all night long!"

Bloody fucking Christ. Simon didn't doubt that she was telling the truth about the horse, but could she have been any more transparent? It was heartwarming, really; especially with what she'd said about the vacant suite of rooms next door to those he shared with Morgan and Jericho.

"I know you don't love me even half as much as I love you, Petal," Simon teased. "As such, go watch the sodding miracle of birth tonight. Just make sure you take a change of clothes. Never seen anything female give birth aside from a cat or twelve, but I do recall that it's not always tidy. Might be even less so when it's something the size of a bloody *horse*!"

Jericho giggled then ran back and jumped up again, this time to peck Simon's cheek with a kiss. "Thanks, Simon! I'm gonna run home and pack! It might be a long labour, though, so don't be surprised if I'm not back before day after tomorrow, okay?"

Simon chuckled and kissed Jericho's cheek in return. "Cook making meatloaf again tomorrow night, then? Go, Petal. We'll miss you, but we'll be happy just knowing you're having fun."

* * * *

"Are you sure he doesn't want us to meet him there?"

Morgan rolled his eyes at hearing the question for the fifth time in as many minutes. "I'm sure, Riv. Si knows his way back here from Med almost as well as he knows his way around insulting Patrice without getting beat for it." He tossed the damp towel that had been around his waist into the corner nearest the bathroom door. "Besides, Simon's been in Med for almost a week and we've gone by to see him every day. What do you think he'd rather have—us collecting him there, or walking in to find you and me naked? This way he doesn't need to worry about undressing anybody but himself."

River laughed at that, which Morgan had to admit was a good look for him. It made those pretty blue eyes sparkle enough that Morgan would have wondered what River was doing with him if Morgan had been a less secure man. As it was, he was thankful that River not only wanted him, but wanted Simon as well.

"True," River said, voice bubbling a bit as he crawled onto the bed. "He does tend to be kind of horny. A lot. Not that I'm saying this is all just sex or anything..."

Morgan hoped not. The last thing the relationship between him, Simon and River was, was 'just sex'. He'd even been sure that River knew it until just then.

Unless River was rethinking things, Morgan realised, which was entirely possible. Morgan didn't like the idea but that didn't mean it wasn't true.

"What are you saying, Riv?" he asked carefully, settling himself naked on the sheets beside the equally nude River. "Because it sounds like you're not sure there's more than sex between all of us and it's kind of pissing me off. And I'm not the best at talking about shit, okay? But if that's what you're thinking, we're about to have a problem." They really, really were.

"What? No!" River sat up, staring from behind a curtain of long blond hair that Morgan figured the guy was using as a shield. "Dude! No fucking way am I saying that! I just..." River looked away and when he spoke again, a second later, his voice was softer. Uncertain. "We fucked, man. You and me. Like...raw. And then all that shit happened with the club and Sky and then Simon was sick and we never...I mean, I'm sure Simon knows about it because how could he not, right? But I don't know how he *feels* about it and it's sort of freaking me out, okay? It's not like he had a chance to say much between finding you, the shit with Moon and Sky on the fucking plane, and getting sick as a dog. I just feel like he might be mad or some shit and I don't know how to deal with it."

The snorting sound coming from the bedroom doorway didn't surprise Morgan. He'd actually heard the main door of the rooms he shared with Rico and Simon open and close while he'd been asking River to clarify the nature of the unconventional relationship between the three of them, sans Rico. He'd also been entirely aware of the fact that it was Simon who'd entered. Rico would have announced herself in her usual manner.

"Bloody hell," Simon said bluntly. "Of all the things you could have brought up while I was in hospital, that's not one you thought to mention? Christ, Riv. How hard is it to say 'shagged your bloke bare, how's that strike you, mate'?"

River made a noise deep in his throat that sounded like a combination of whine and whimper, and when Morgan turned his head to look towards the door he understood why. A remarkably similar sound left *him* at the sight of Simon standing there, naked and hard.

Simon smirked, moving into the room with a feline grace Morgan could only envy, as usual. "Can't tell me you two haven't been going at it whilst I've been laid up, either. Comes down to it, thinking about the two of you rolling about, no latex between you, was what got me through the stunningly boring nights, yeah?"

The next thing Morgan knew, Simon was at the foot of the bed. Then Simon crawled up the mattress, sliding between him and River as though Simon's DNA was skewing towards the big-cat side instead of human. It was fucking sexy, just like always, and possibly more so owing to the fact that it had been so long since Morgan had seen Simon do that.

"Oh, man," River breathed, sounding awe-struck, and Morgan couldn't blame him. There was something about Simon prowling that was definitely inspiring. Exciting. Sensual and sexual, though those things didn't always go together.

They went together perfectly where Simon was concerned, though, and Morgan truly couldn't believe that he'd actually forgotten that during the Game and the following days without Simon. "Oh, man," he echoed.

"Hell with all that 'oh, man' crap, loves." Simon smirked. "I'm here, we're all starkers..." Then Simon's smirk faded. Morgan doubted that River had noticed, but after as much time as Morgan had spent cataloguing Simon's every expression, *he'd* seen it. "Doc says I'm fine. How do you blokes feel about that?"

"You're so far beyond just 'fine', I don't think there's even a word for it," Morgan murmured as he leaned in and plastered his lips to his lover's. His first lover's, really, because River was there too, and he definitely counted.

* * * *

Simon standing naked in the doorway had been almost too hot for River to stand. Simon's sinuous progress from door to bed, then the equally slinky slither to push between him and Morgan was one of those things River wished he had video footage for, to go along with the memory. Watching Morgan plundering Simon's mouth and the way Simon reacted, though...that was the hottest thing River had ever seen.

He'd been in bed with both of them before, but there was something about the way Simon and Morgan connected after time apart that was just too erection-inducing for words. He almost felt like he was intruding, but only almost because Simon stretched one hand out, finding River's side, and River couldn't feel like he was anything but welcome right where he was when Simon's fingers splayed, stroking over skin.

Simon's eyes were closed, but Morgan's weren't. Morgan was actually looking right at him, River saw. Looking with such heat and desire, River couldn't doubt that whatever was happening, he was a needed part of it.

It was a little bit weird that he was so comfortable in a relationship with two other men. Not because they were men but because River had always figured that he would settle down someday with just one other person. He'd never had any sort of preference as to whether that person would be male or female, but he'd never really considered the idea that he would be lucky enough to find *two* people who cared about him and about each other and still have room for one more, yet there he was. He kept waiting for Simon and Morgan to change their minds about him but they hadn't and now that Simon was out of Med and seemed happy to keep the three of them together, River wasn't willing to doubt any more.

Yes, he and Morgan had gone at it more than once without condoms and that was a really big deal, but there had still been a chance that Simon might change his mind, or so River had thought. Thought wrongly.

"Dude," River said, one hand sliding over Simon's hair to tangle in Morgan's, "I want my turn with that mouth, too. I haven't kissed Simon in months!"

Morgan laughed, his eyes sparkling with amusement. "Try days, baby. But go for it. I haven't had his cock in my mouth since before the Game, and that's a fucking tragedy!"

"Right, then." Simon broke in before River could respond. "Can I just say I'm the luckiest bloke on the planet? Because I am. Now proceed. Mouths on me. Right now would work just fine."

River didn't have a single thing to say to that. Instead of speaking he simply laughed and laid himself down, half on Simon and half on the bed. Then he pressed his lips to Simon's, groaning softly when Simon's tongue slid over his lips then into his mouth.

Oh, yeah. There was no way he, Simon and Morgan were anything but real. No way at all.

Chapter Fourteen

Bloody fucking hell. Simon couldn't manage to think any more clearly than that or even find another thought to have. He wasn't even trying, really.

He was in bed with his first real love, Morgan, while his second real love plundered his mouth as though it was a cave and River was spelunking.

Simon's mouth was occupied with the way River was exploring it, but he was still fully aware of Morgan's lips. He felt every moment, every slide of soft warmth against his shoulder, his chest. He moaned a little bit, though River swallowed it, when Morgan latched on to one nipple, teasing it with tongue and teeth, and Simon moaned again at the thought that Morgan had likely done just that to River when Simon hadn't been around to see it. He knew for a fact that River was a responsive lover, and while it felt odd to not be jealous, Simon wasn't. Not even a little.

So Morgan had spent time alone with River while Simon had been laid up. His blokes had enjoyed each other without him in the mix. It should have been distressing, at the very least, but...no.

Then Morgan's soft, aggressive lips moved lower and Simon lost himself in the sensation of having his mouth taken while also being teased in a way that wouldn't have been possible with just the one bloke.

Lips on his own, River's tongue claiming his mouth with an intensity Simon adored. Morgan's mouth sealing around his navel while Morgan's mobile tongue teased that indentation rhythmically. River's hands roaming, finding every spot the bloke had discovered during the many times Simon and Morgan had spent with River.

It was mind-blowing and hotter than sin, and Simon would know. Sin had been his forte at one point. He'd had sex for money, back before the FGC, but that didn't matter in any sense, except that it allowed him to recognise the difference between fucking and making love.

Simon groaned softly as River's lips moved from his own, then he made a sound even he couldn't quantify because that mouth found the side of his neck instead, and Simon would never admit it out loud, but he loved it when a bloke played at his neck. Which River clearly remembered from all the time they'd done exactly what they were doing, before.

Except it wasn't 'exactly', was it?

Things had changed in Prague. Changed immensely. The situation there had led Morgan to up the ante with River, and Simon was fine with that. They — the three of them — worked together in a way that had nothing to do with the FGC and everything to do with emotional fulfilment. Love, if it had to have a defining word.

Simon barely noticed it when Morgan pulled away, but Morgan's return made more than a slight impact because that return was accompanied by slick fingers pushing between the cheeks of his ass.

"Bloody hell! Been too long, love!" It really had. Simon was surprised, but also not, that he'd missed the sensation of Morgan's fingers delving into him. It wasn't that he'd forgotten how it felt to be slicked and opened for Morgan's cock, but between the Game and the physical rehab...yeah. He'd missed it, for fuck's sake.

Morgan did something. Shifted in a way Simon didn't understand at first, but then River's mouth on Simon's neck lifted and River released a shuddering breath. "Oh, yeah! More, baby!" He assumed River meant Morgan because River had never called Simon 'baby'.

"I'd have your cock in my mouth right now, Si," Morgan said bluntly, still stretching Simon enough that Simon couldn't speak, "but I have this whole vision in mind. Me inside you, you inside Riv. That's where I want you to come right now. Not in my mouth. We'll do that later, okay?"

It was so much better than merely 'okay' that Simon couldn't answer even if he'd wanted to. Fortunately, neither of his blokes seemed to mind. Then River stroked over his torso again and found his nipples, teasing and taunting and pinching, and Simon lost what little was left of his mind. Happily.

* * * *

There was something about making love to Simon — with River — while knowing it was making love rather than just fucking, that was so far beyond satisfying that Morgan didn't quite know what to call it. It was more than pleasing, more than enjoyable...it was even more than perfect, though Morgan had never suspected that there *was* anything more than perfect. Perfect was meant to be the ultimate, but being with both Simon and River and knowing that what the three of them shared was true and sincere took things to a whole other level.

It was maybe a little bit sad that Morgan hadn't realised just how much he cared for River until Prague. He'd known that he cared for the guy, yes, but it had only been when he'd thought River was lost to him that Morgan had known for sure that he loved the boy. Boy might not be the right word, really, because River was twenty-four — almost twenty-five — but still, Morgan couldn't help thinking of him as the kid in the relationship. River's age didn't have any sort of detrimental effect on how much Morgan loved River, though.

He'd done his best to show River while Simon had been sequestered in the Med Centre, but he hadn't said the words. It just hadn't felt right to do it without Simon there too, because Morgan suspected that Simon felt it just as much as he did himself. Not that it mattered right then, when Morgan had three fingers of one hand sliding in and out of Simon's ass and two fingers of the other, equally slick, opening River.

It was a delicate balancing act. Not just having his hands engaged, but managing to keep himself from hurting either of his men. His position was precarious, at best, with only one elbow supporting him, and that wasn't going to last long. Still, Morgan had a feeling about how things needed to play out, and when that feeling intensified, he went with it.

"I need you on your hands and knees, River," he said simply. "Because I'm definitely going to be inside Si while he's inside you, so that'll be easiest for all of us."

River's laugh was slightly muffled, and when Morgan looked up he saw that it was Simon's shoulder that had blocked the full sound.

"Dude. Does that mean I finally get to feel Simon fuck me bare?" River seemed to already know the answer, though, because he pulled away and assumed the position, waggling his ass a little after a second or so.

"No," Simon answered before Morgan could. "Means you're about to be made love to, you git."

Morgan tried not to laugh, but he couldn't help it. When River looked back over one shoulder, all that blond hair trailing over the other to pool on the mattress, Morgan lost it. He laughed harder than he'd done in weeks.

"It means you're going to be non-verbal in about a minute. Simon without a rubber is just that good."

* * * *

Oh, God. Morgan hadn't been kidding.

Just the way Simon's dick felt pushing into him, natural and naked, had River ready to spill. He'd never had anyone inside him without a condom other than Morgan, and Morgan and Simon were a package deal, which River had known when he'd first hooked up with them. Except 'hooked up' wasn't the right term any more. River was sure of that much.

They'd connected, even before the Prague Game. They'd even agreed that outside of Games they were a thing. Right then, post-Prague, River didn't want to have that whole 'other than Games' exclusion. Then Simon was grasping his hips and River felt the bulbous tip of Simon's cock pushing harder at his hole and it was different. So fucking different from the last time he'd had Simon.

"I. Can you…" River was ashamed of his own tentative tone, but he felt oddly fragile right then. "Can you go slow? It's just…this is *real*, y'know?"

"I can go as slow as you need me to, love," Simon murmured, and that was enough to have River melting. "You'll tell me if I'm hurting you, yeah?"

Fuck yes. He would. Except, "I know you'd never hurt me. Not if you could help it. I. Okay. Faster is good, now. I'm ready."

River didn't change his mind, even when Simon surged forward, pushing his thick tip through. He gasped, but he didn't change his mind. It was sudden and stunning but not painful, really. Simon's cock wasn't as big around as Morgan's but it was longer. River thought he felt it in his throat. Then Simon stilled, buried balls-deep inside him, and River felt pressure, though not from Simon, in some odd way.

Simon was sure of only one thing, once he'd managed to restrain the impulse to slam roughly into River's entirely too tempting body. He was sure that if Morgan didn't hurry the fuck up, Simon might just blow his own load before his bloke even got in him. It wasn't a happy realisation and did nothing to shore up Simon's quickly fading, entirely underdeveloped sense of patience, but there it was. He needed this. Needed to be Simon-in-the-middle this first time they were all connected this way.

"Come on, love. Move your stunning yet lagging ass, yeah?" Morgan had better.

Morgan laughed from behind him, and Simon
spared a moment to consider taking umbrage, but
then the bed shifted and mere seconds later, Morgan
was pressing against him, cock huge and hard,
insistent enough that Simon held his breath while the
broad, lube-slicked head pushed inside.

"Bloody fucking *yes!*" Simon groaned, the force of
Morgan's entry shoving Simon's own cock harder into
River. Harder but not deeper, Simon was sure,
because he'd already shored up against heated,
smooth skin, his sac right there brushing River's. "Just
like that, love, but do your blokes a proper and give it
a moment, yeah? Be a shame if I shot off without a
single thrust, and I just might." True enough,
considering how intense it all was. Him in River, that
hot, tight sheath of man so tight around him...and
Morgan in *him*, big fat cock stretching Simon open just
right. He was familiar with both sensations, granted,
but Simon hadn't realised that to experience both at
once would have him feeling so desperate. Desperate
to come, and equally eager to have the experience last
forever. Or maybe just minutes. Whichever. More than
the ten seconds it had been, in any case.

Morgan moaned. Simon felt it against his shoulder
just as much as he heard it, but Morgan paused, barely
moving at all. "Tell me it's been a moment, Si,"
Morgan muttered and Simon thought about laughing
but he didn't. Couldn't when he heard his own needy,
wanton desire reflected in Morgan's voice.

"Yeah. Yeah," he grated out. "Do it, love. Let me feel
it."

Another moan against Simon's shoulder and he
gasped roughly as Morgan surged forward, driving
the rest of that thick, hot cock deep. He gasped again
when Morgan reversed the motion, pulling back

slowly enough that Simon felt every single ridge and vein of that glorious prick, it seemed like.

"Hold on to your hat, pet," he murmured against River's neck. "Think our bloke's about to go wild on the both of us."

"Dude!" That was the only recognisable word River spoke, but his tone was anticipatory rather than reluctant, and that was all Simon needed to understand. Then Morgan shoved deep again, and Simon groaned. Morgan pulled back and Simon did too, slowly, doing his best to make sure River felt every moment.

It was different. It shouldn't have been, because Morgan had for damned sure fucked Simon from behind before, but it was definitely different right then. Knowing River was in front of Simon, just as speared by Simon's cock as Simon was by Morgan's *made* it different.

Morgan's heart was racing even more than it usually did when he was naked with his two guys, but then again, this time Morgan was doing more than making love to Simon. He was also making love to River, even though it was through Simon's body. Fuck, they were all making love. It didn't much matter who was in who. What mattered was the three of them together, in whatever combination. Together, with the knowledge that they weren't just 'a thing', that they were much more than casual.

He wasn't ready to say it yet, but he knew he loved them both. Not in the same way, exactly, and not equally. Not yet. But Morgan could absolutely imagine a time in the future when he would know deep down inside that he couldn't choose between the two men who'd stolen parts of his heart. That made it even more important that he show them what he felt, even without announcing it.

He thrust roughly for a few more seconds, then slowed in the face of the orgasm hurtling towards him. He wasn't ready for this to be over yet. Wasn't even close to it. He wouldn't last forever, of course, but a few more minutes would be good. Just long enough to get River off. Long enough to feel Simon shuddering when he spilled deep inside River's body. Then Morgan could come, too. Just fill Simon right the fuck up, probably so much that the tight ass wrapped around Morgan's cock would overflow.

Fuck, a few more minutes would be God damn perfect.

Oh, Lord. I could die right now and be happy about it. It was the most coherent thought River had had since Simon's advice to hold on to his hat. Even then, he'd thought something like *I don't have a hat but even if I did, I'd be willing to lose it for this*, but he hadn't been able to verbalise it.

His entire body was already sore, but it was the kind of soreness that River treasured. The kind that said he was being loved to within an inch of too much. It wasn't a sensation he'd known until he'd formed his odd relationship with Morgan and Simon, and it hadn't just appeared one day, fully formed. River honestly didn't have any idea about when it had started, but it had grown and flourished and continued to do so. It was a good feeling. It was more than good a moment later, when Simon wrapped one strong hand around River's cock.

"Urrr!" It wasn't a word, but it was all River could manage. Hell, he was surprised he'd had any breath to even make that sound, what with the way Simon and Morgan were moving, their pace picking up, Simon's cock forcing each breath from River's lungs as their unexpectedly synchronised loving continued. Then Simon started sliding that talented hand on River's shaft and River lost the rhythm they'd fallen into, his body bucking as much as it could with the partial weight of his two dudes on him.

"That's it, pet. Give it up for me." How the hell was Simon even able to speak?

Morgan grunted something, River didn't know what, and then the pace from behind became faster, harder, and Simon made a noise that was part stuttered cry and part shaky wail, as far as River could tell, and that was more like it. He was glad that Morgan had taken it upon himself to push Simon into the non-verbal arena where he and Morgan had already been. Happier still that Simon started fisting his cock even more quickly, doing that little brush-and-palm-rub over his tip that River loved so much.

After that, it was all sweating and writhing and rocking for River. It was all about coming while Simon plundered his ass, and Morgan apparently plundered Simon's.

River didn't know how much he could claim, really, but by the time Simon came in him, followed closely by Morgan spilling rough and hard inside Simon — River honestly believed that Simon and Morgan wanted him for good, and there was no way that was a bad thing.

River fell asleep wrapped in strong arms, still covered in his own spunk. He couldn't quite manage to worry about that, either. The only thing he regretted about the entire evening was that he hadn't managed to suck off his lovers.

Then again, there was always the morning. River could deal with that.

* * * *

Mental note. River needs to tie up his sodding hair before we pass out, from now on.

The thought made Simon laugh and nearly swallow a few long blond strands, which only made the notion more sincere. He loved River's hair. Loved the way it slid over him like weighted silk, and the way it lashed and stroked his skin when he, Morgan and River were in the midst of things was nothing short of being entirely brilliant. That didn't mean Simon wanted to inhale it. He'd likely end up like a cat who'd accidentally eaten Christmas tinsel.

Simon laughed again, though this time it was from imagining himself scooting along the carpeting, dragging his ass against the fibres in an attempt to dislodge the irritant from his bum. He'd actually had a cat once who'd got into the tinsel and it hadn't been pretty or pleasant for the cat.

Morgan shifted a little and Simon was just in time to see those beautiful brown eyes open. "What's so funny?" Morgan muttered, and Simon could only grin at the sight of his two loves curled together. It was likely even more glorious to see from a few feet away, but fuck if Simon was going to leave the bed and the warmth of his blokes just to have a look-see. He could do that later, he figured, or maybe get whatever footage they had down in tech division from the hours just past.

Even so, he wasn't willing to truly lie to Morgan, so Simon told part of the truth. Not the tinsel-cat's-ass portion, but close enough.

"I was just thinking, love. Hate to wake up some time and find one of us strangled in our sleep by our bloke's hair, yeah? Talk about ignominious ends. And it'd likely have him feeling all guilty and whatnot."

Morgan's slow blink told Simon that he was truly awake, as did the one big, tanned hand that relocated from River's side to Simon's hip as Morgan peered at him over River's lax form. "You want him to cut his hair?" Morgan sounded horrified.

Simon snorted. "Only if he wants to, love. I've become something of a fan of all that golden shimmer. Just thinking, is all." He grinned again and Morgan smiled, the horror leaving his eyes.

"Good," Morgan answered quietly, fingers flexing on Simon's skin just enough that Simon felt it. "I love his hair. Love him more, but still. His hair is like...fuck if I know how to say this without sounding stupid, but his hair is like us. The three of us."

That made absolutely no sense yet, but Simon was sure Morgan would get around to explaining it, once the man finished yawning. Morgan wasn't always good with the talking—hell, neither was Simon—but he generally got to the point eventually, and it was usually a good one.

"You and I," Morgan finally said, still softly; presumably out of deference to their sleeping love, Simon figured, "we work, Si. But we're a lot alike, in a lot of ways. Riv's different. He's...pure, I guess, in a way neither of us has been since we were younger than he is now. He's our foil, maybe. He makes us more and better, just by being with us. He's our joy, maybe?"

Well, on the one hand, Morgan might be right. Bringing River into the relationship had definitely changed the dynamic. Simon couldn't deny that he and Morgan were more serious about things than River tended to be, and while River could absolutely be all about the Game when they were in the field, the young blond also had a certain devil-may-care attitude that balanced them out well.

On the other hand, Simon had never thought that 'joy' was lacking in his relationship with Morgan, pre-River. It was more than a little bit insulting that Morgan seemed to think they'd been missing that. They'd been more than happy together before River, hadn't they?

Some of that must have shown on his face because Morgan, enormous git that he was, suddenly spoke again.

"Sorry. That's the wrong word." Morgan was frowning and Simon couldn't blame him. "I just realised how that sounded. It's not... Okay, it's like he somehow makes things seem brighter when he's with us. You and I see the darkness, Si. It's part of who we are and that works for us, you know? But when we're with River, he sort of dilutes that. For me, anyway. He makes me see the light all around us."

Simon sighed. Quietly, because he didn't want to wake River any more than Morgan did. He couldn't even say Morgan was wrong. "For a bloke who's not big with words, you seem to have said that much more plainly than I would have expected." Truer words were never spoken. "But what the bloody fuck does that have to do with his hair being like us?" That was the part Simon didn't get. At all.

River grumbled unexpectedly then and turned just enough to look at Simon over one shoulder that Simon wanted to lick, just like that. "Means it wraps all around you guys and ties us together, even if it's weird for a guy to have so much hair. Now shut up or blow me, okay? I could sleep more, but I could also go for a blowjob. Up to you."

* * * *

Simon's mouth on his cock while Morgan ate his ass? Oh, that was something River wanted to do again and again; no question. But there was something really pleasurable about being in the big-ass shower stall with his own urges temporarily satisfied that River found equally enticing. There was a certain simplicity to sliding his lather-coated hands over Morgan's chest while Simon soaped him from behind that River truly enjoyed.

It was the first time they'd done this, really. The first time they'd spent ages just touching, hands moving more or less innocently over each other's skin without any expectation of sexual intimacy or the tension that sort of expectation created.

It was the first time River had showered with anyone while knowing that it was just showering. The first time it hadn't been a build-up—or coming-down—that was going to lead to sex, and it was awesome. Free.

He felt more than slightly stupid for thinking of freedom while surrounded by the guys he was sleeping with, their hands so possessive, but it was true. For the first time in his life, River felt free and easy while his own touch made River's ownership of both his men equally clear.

Morgan's chest. Firm and strong. Bulging just a bit with muscle. Abs like cobblestones, hard beneath his fingers. Glutes without more than an ounce of fat—just enough to have those dimples at the sides where River's fingertips seemed to rest more often than not.

And Simon.

Leaner than Morgan, but no less toned. Just the far side of slender, Simon's body was ripped without being bulky. Defined muscles, small pecs that felt so very right when River skated his soap-slicked hands over them, and Simon's torso... God, if River were the sort to write sonnets, he could have penned volumes about the way Simon's skin twitched when River touched it. Entire tomes would have been dedicated to the sensations of Simon's muscles against his palms, and Morgan's, as well.

River wasn't a poet, though, and he wasn't even willing to try, so all he could do was moan and sigh happily at the slow, sensual touches he gave and received, and maybe he wasn't as sated as he'd thought. His body was for damned sure trying to rally again.

Moments later, with Morgan pressed against his front and Simon plastered to his back, River discovered that yes, it was entirely possible for two guys older than he was to recover faster...and yes, shower sex was still amazing when it was him with Simon and Morgan. Thank God.

* * * *

Oh, Christ. Morgan's entire body was on lock-down, it felt like. Then again, he'd had more sex in the last twelve hours than he'd had in...he didn't know. A month or two?

Whatever. He was all fucked out, in any case. That last round in the shower had completely done him in.

Fortunately, Simon and River seemed to be just as wrung out as Morgan was, physically. The unfortunate part was that Morgan had slept just enough that his brain was going a mile a minute. Or maybe only a foot a second. He couldn't be sure. But he was thinking and it was harshing his post-orgasmic buzz, as River would say, damn it.

"I love you." The words came from him without any intention of speaking, but Morgan meant them. He couldn't pretend he didn't. "Both of you," he clarified, because what was that saying? In for a penny, in for a pound? Yeah, that was how he felt. He didn't necessarily love Simon and River equally, but he did love them both. Enough that losing either of them might wreck him. *Would* wreck him. "I just needed to say it."

Morgan wasn't sure, but it might even be the first time he'd said it to Simon, though he had no doubt that they'd known it the entire time they'd been together. Simon wasn't the sort to need the words, though. River...well, Morgan had a feeling that River *was*.

Simon's chuckle wasn't a shock. "Imagine that," Simon uttered, sounding playful. "Boy scout's in love with the blokes he's sleeping with. Colour me shocked." Then Simon smiled against River's chest and Morgan saw those pretty eyes dart up to meet his own. "Pretty sure you know the sentiment is returned, you daft bugger, but if you were at all wondering, it is."

River was a bit less reserved in his answer, though he didn't leap up or anything. Instead, he raised his free hand—the one that wasn't curved over Simon's hip—and Morgan nearly moaned at the sensation of River's palm against his cheek.

"I love you, too," River said, blunt and bold as day. "I do. You and Simon. And I don't know how we're going to make this work, but we will. I mean, you guys have Keeta—I mean Jericho—and she might have a problem with things if it's all three of us, but I want to make this work and if we can, then maybe... I don't know. I just... I love you. Both."

Morgan hadn't actually considered what Rico would make of having River brought into the mix. He should have, but he hadn't. It had been one thing when he and Simon had thought River might be a passing fancy, but River wasn't anything like that. Not any more.

"Don't think we need to worry much about that, loves," Simon said before Morgan could respond. "Petal's a bright girl. Came to see me earlier and said..."

Morgan knew he was blushing while Simon went on, but he couldn't help it. He also couldn't deny that Rico had come up with the perfect solution.

If River took the next-door suite and they put a door in, between that suite and Morgan and Simon's bedroom, things would be just about perfect.

They would have time to ease people into the idea of him, Simon and River being a threesome, as well as time to discover whether they would truly work out as a trio and a family, where Rico was concerned. It would be much better than just moving River in and hoping for the best.

Morgan relaxed and wrapped one arm over Simon and River. "I think we can work with that. All of us."

River made a sound that clearly agreed, then Simon cleared his throat. "Suppose I should tell you the rest of what Princess said. Not sure how you'll react, but...figure you need to know. It's a secret and we need to keep it that way for a bit, yeah?"

Morgan wasn't sure about why Simon thought anything spoken inside the FGC HQ could be kept secret, but he was willing to listen. So was River, it seemed...up to a point. Then it just got ugly. Ugly enough that Morgan figured tech division would send a security team, but that didn't happen.

Then again, Morgan realised an hour or so later, tech division usually blanked out when there was sex going on…and he, Simon and River had definitely been having sex. The screaming would probably have registered as very similar.

Chapter Fifteen

Bloody hell. Simon didn't have a single fucking clue about why River had reacted so violently, in the emotional sense, to Sky being on the fringes of the FGC's above-ground complex. It wasn't as though the bloke could gain access to the actual HQ, was it?

Yet the seemingly simple words "Princess says your brother's camped out at the house past the third pond" had resulted in Riv losing his proverbial shit.

Maybe it was that River couldn't believe his brother had managed to trail them from the airstrip without having resources in the United States. Simon could understand that. It was a fair bit disturbing, after all. The idea that someone who wasn't associated with the FGC had located the Club all on their own? Yeah, 'disturbing' didn't even begin to cover it.

Nonetheless, Jericho had said Sky wasn't a danger to them, and while Simon might doubt the girl's taste in clothes and shoes and friends—Petal liked spending time with bitchy-bitch Patrice, after all—Jericho had never been wrong when it mattered. Simon trusted her to a degree that would seem bizarre to anyone who didn't know her. After all, she was a twelve-year-old girl. Most people outside the Club wouldn't have any clue about her unique abilities, but Simon did. He'd thought River was aware, as well, but the argument they'd had that night in bed, naked as the days they were born, hadn't supported that theory.

Three days later, Simon still didn't know where he stood.

He trusted Jericho. Trusted her 'senses' to steer him right. But he also trusted River, and River had said Sky was dangerous. The question was whether Sky was dangerous to the FGC or merely to other people. *Bad* people, as the FGC reckoned 'bad' with regards to people in general.

It was an interesting question, really. What constituted 'bad'? Was it political beliefs, personal strictures, or actions? If a person *knew* something was wrong but didn't stop it, or stop themselves from doing it, did that make them 'bad'? Was 'immoral' the same as 'bad' even when someone didn't share the same belief system?

Simon knew what *he* believed, but he didn't have a single clue about what River truly considered to be 'bad', did he? And that was exactly why he was wandering around up on the Ranch, out by the house beyond the third pond.

He wasn't there to confront Sky, as such. He honestly hadn't formed an opinion. He was definitely skewed towards believing River, but Jericho's words carried almost as much weight, even though she was just a child and could be mistaken — owing to hormones, maybe. She was at that age, after all.

Simon sat at the end of the tiny dock that stretched out into the relatively small pond. There was a decayed rowboat tied up to it with maybe three strands of twisted rope left. The rowboat itself was sunk into the mud that proved the water was drying up, but that wasn't unusual for the time of year. It had been a long, hot summer without enough rain.

He removed his shoes, rolled up the ends of his jeans, and dangled his feet in the water that barely covered his feet to the ankles, and Simon deliberately didn't react when he heard and felt the cat-soft footsteps coming up behind him on the dock.

"So he sent *you*."

The tone was accusatory, but Simon only laughed. Just a little and not for long, but he laughed. "Not even a little bit, mate. Riv would likely try to kill me if he knew I was here. He'd fail, by the way. I'm still better than him at hand to hand. My step-daughter sent me this way, if you must know." Simon chuckled again. "That would be your brother's adopted child, assuming all goes well with me, my bloke and River."

River's brother was silent for a good twenty seconds. Simon knew because he counted them out in his head.

"I'm not here to make trouble for him."

Simon nodded slowly. "Right, then. Pull up a bit of dock and tell me why you *are* here. I came out unarmed and such, just so I could get your perspective. Even though River says you're a dangerous man, and for someone in the FGC to say that? Bloody well disturbing, yeah?"

The next thing Simon knew, his second love's brother was sitting beside him at the end of the dock, bare feet splashing the water, as well.

"You know the only reason he says that is because I killed Moony's first boyfriend, right?"

It was so matter-of-fact that Simon didn't know how to respond.

"We were seventeen," Sky went on, "and he drugged her. Even so, our dad spent most of our lives exposing us to various chemicals, so she wasn't as out of it as her so-called 'boyfriend' hoped. I heard her telling him no, and I heard him ignoring her 'no' so I did what needed to be done." Sky sighed loudly. "I might have been a little more violent than necessary, but no one ever found the body parts and I promise you that when Moon did lose her virginity, it was because she wanted to. Not because some fucking asshole decided it was his *right* to take it from her just because he paid for a few movies."

"A *little* more violent?" Simon laughed. "Just a little? There were body parts."

Sky sounded smug. He even looked it when Simon dared a glance at the bloke.

"I might have accidentally cut his head off. The lower one. And then the upper one, less accidentally. And I'd do it again. She's my twin sister. We shared a womb. How could I do anything less when she was on the edge of being raped?"

Twin sister. That was the part that still had Simon baffled, just as Morgan had been in Prague. The rest of it he could understand. Well, not the whole chopping someone's willy off, or someone's head, but the desire to destroy someone who'd tried to harm someone he loved? Yeah. He got that. But…twin?

He must have said some of that out loud because Sky answered.

"Mom wasn't the sort to be pregnant all the time, so when she found out there were three of us she was fucking ecstatic. River and I…we're identical twins. Shared an egg and everything. Moon, though…? She's a girl. Okay, she looks a lot like us, and she's our twin, but River is my *real* twin. Moon is my other twin.

Three kids at once, three sets of twins. Me and River, River and Moon, Moon and me."

Okay, that made an odd sort of sense, even while it didn't make any sense at all, but sod it. If Sky wanted to delude himself, then whatever. Except not 'whatever' because River thought Sky was dangerous and, from what Sky had said, the bloke actually was.

If River, Moon and Sky truly had all been born at the same time, then Sky had not only decapitated someone, but cut off their pecker as well. At seventeen. That was truly frightening.

Sky was definitely dangerous, but Simon couldn't conclude that it translated as bad right then. Unless someone tried to rape Moon again, of course, in which case Simon pitied the bloke who did because if Moon didn't kill him herself, Sky apparently would.

"So you're not here to fuck with things, then." Because that was what Simon had garnered from the conversation, aside from all the personally relevant things since he was involved with River. "Why the bloody fuck *are* you here? Not in the U.S., but here-here? Unless you're thinking the Russians won't follow you."

Sky turned away and it was only then, with the setting sun reflecting from the bloke's cheekbones, that Simon realised Sky had taken all the jewellery out of his face.

The hair was still long and black. The eyebrows still matched the darkness of the hair. But in that moment Simon saw just how identical Sky was to River.

"You dye it."

"No shit, Sherlock." Sky was unapologetic, at best. "And I stopped here just to have some downtime, but I'm thinking I might stick around a while, now that I've sort of met someone. My hair can grow out, if that's what it takes. I don't think he's even noticed that I'm not River. Can you... I know you don't have any reason to help me, but will you? It's Simon, right? Will you help me get to know Zeke, or at least clue me to his story?"

Oh, bloody hell. Not even a small possibility of that. The meeting or the sharing.

Simon finally had everything he'd ever wanted and River's brother wanted to know Zeke? With something in Sky's tone that implied he wanted to 'get to know' the big, lumbering man in the biblical way? That could screw things up beyond the telling of it. And Zeke...well, Zeke would never be able to handle Sky. Not even slightly.

"Sorry, mate." Simon actually was sorry, in a way he couldn't explain. "Zeke isn't available. Might be best to just gather yourself here at the pond house for a bit and move on."

Sky sighed, finally sounding as young as his siblings to Simon. "You could be right. I'm just not sure that I can. Look, the thing in Prague... Well, I was trying to help. I really was. Mom always told me that if I couldn't help people I might as well just live under a rock. It's pretty clear that the whole thing ended badly. I trusted some people I shouldn't have." Sky cleared his throat. "Thanks for not handing me over to the Russians, by the way. That was really cool of you."

It was only then, when Sky said 'really cool of you' that Simon knew he would never be able to run Sky off. The bloke sounded far too much like River. Looked far too much like him as the last, lingering rays of sun touched that dyed-black hair and painted it red-gold.

"Not a problem," Simon said, but then he snorted. "Actually, it's been a huge fucking issue. Still, nobody outside the Club knows where you are or even suspects that we had anything to do with your 'miraculous' disappearance. If it's any consolation, it seems that the Russians haven't retaken the Cern Oblocha Bar. That oddly flexible twink who kicked my bloke Morgan in the chin appears to be in charge. So far, anyway."

Sky looked a slight bit baffled, as far as Simon could tell. It only lasted for a second or so but Simon saw it before Sky quirked an odd little half-grin.

"That would be Dmitri. I always knew that kid was smarter than he let on. So Zeke really isn't single?"

Bloody fucking hell. Sky sounded so hopeful that Simon knew the poor bloke was unaware of it. Even with as small as his own acquaintance with the boy was — and boy was something of a stretch, considering what Simon knew of Sky — the younger man sounded just that. Hopeful.

Even worse was that Simon couldn't bring himself to lie to River's brother, though lying would be the smart thing to do. The *right* thing. Zeke was damaged and borderline psychotic, some days. But Zeke was also on a course of meds Doc Pritchard had dreamed up that kept the truly huge and intensely scarred man sane enough to act as a perimeter guard around the FGC's top-side operation. And Jericho adored Zeke, which was another tick for the plus column.

"Bloke's had a rough go of it," Simon finally said. "And he's got a truly unlikely number of friends here. Might be best if you just keep things as light as they are and move on soon, yeah? Best for you, I mean. Nobody up on the Ranch takes it lightly when blokes mess with Zeke. They take it even worse down below, if you want to know the truth. He's one of my step-daughter's favourite people, and that's saying a lot, though I suppose it doesn't mean much of anything to you. Believe me when I say the last thing you want to do is get into Petal's bad graces."

Sky looked like he was thinking about it, and Simon let him. It was fair enough to assume that it might take a short while to process the information that screwing about with Zeke could easily have a truly large number of highly trained people who knew exactly how to kill a man gunning for one's ass, after all. Then again, Sky apparently knew how to kill people—and decapitate them—just as well, so who knew?

"Fine," Sky answered with a sigh that Simon couldn't call sincere. He'd heard enough of River's fake capitulation to recognise the similar tone. "I'll just regroup for a few days and head off to...wherever. I know enough of my dad's old contacts; at least I do if any of them are still alive. It's not like I can't find things to do for money. Just...can you tell River and Moon that I love them? That I never stopped thinking about them? They're the only family I have left, what with Mom going missing in Tibet a few months ago."

Missing? That was news to Simon. Then again, it had been ages since River, at least, had heard from his mum. Even so, Simon wasn't convinced that Sky Stone could possibly know something the Club didn't, when it related to the parent of not one but two Members. He made a mental note to have someone in tech or research look into it. Perhaps both.

"I'll give them the message, though I'll likely tell them you've already left for parts unknown. Can't speak for Moony, but River..." Simon let his voice trail off, not sure how to say it.

"River still thinks I'm the antichrist." Sky seemed amused. "He would. He works with you guys now, so he must have become a lot more morally flexible than he was when I left him and Moon, but inside? He still remembers me as the guy who did all that shit to Moon's ex. He thought I was a monster, but he still helped me hide the body...body *parts*." Sky chuckled mirthlessly. "That's enough to let me at least hope he'll come around eventually."

Simon snorted. He couldn't help it. He not only snorted but arched a very sceptical brow at Sky. "You *have* met your brother, right? A more stubborn pillock hasn't yet been born. Sure, he comes off as being all New Age, mellow, latter-day hippy-ish, but I've yet to see him change his mind about anything what mattered. I'm not saying it'll never happen, but..."

"But magic eight ball says 'outlook not so good'?" Sky nodded. "I know. It doesn't matter what he thinks of me. If he ever needs me, I'm there. Moon, too."

Simon sighed and pulled his feet from the pond water, then stood on the end of the dock, looking down at Sky in the steadily dimming light. "I'll tell them. But with regards to what you said, mate. About having contacts and such?"

Sky nodded and stood, as well.

"I hope it never happens," Simon went on, "but if I ever come up against you on a job and you turn out to be a danger to me or those I care for? I won't hesitate to end you. Morgan would hesitate. River likely would too, and Moon. They're better people than I'll ever be, the lot of them. Call it fair warning, yeah?"

Sky laughed and this time he definitely sounded amused, or possibly just happy. "Glad to hear it. Because if anything happens to River or Moon while they're part of your team and I find out it's your fault? There won't even be body parts for your people to find."

* * * *

"He threatened you?" Morgan was about a moment away from storming out of their rooms and tracking down fucking Sky for it. He wasn't sure whether he'd kill the jackass—probably wouldn't, since Sky was River's brother—or just beat the ever-loving shit out of him, but he would have done one or the other, except for the fact that Morgan was naked and wet right then.

Simon snorted and tilted his head back under the spray from the shower. The length of Simon's neck distracted Morgan from the fury racing through him. "Please, love. Threatened him first, didn't I? Can't blame the bloke for making it clear that it goes both ways. He hurts you lot and I hurt him. I do something that leads to...well, not all of you, but River or Moon being hurt, he hurts me. It's all very civilised, really. Now get your invisible knickers out of their twist for me. Sky and I have an understanding, is all."

Morgan couldn't hold back the grumble that built in his chest and begged for release. "I don't get how you can be so okay with it," he admitted when the rumbling had faded. "He has a history of chopping people into parts! You said so yourself!"

"One person. Some prat who was trying to rape Moony. The bloke has hardly left a trail of dismembered bodies lying about over the last six years." Simon stepped from beneath the spray and Morgan took that as a sign that it was his turn to rinse the conditioner from his hair.

"Never had a sister," Simon went on, and while the water pouring over him muffled the sound slightly, Morgan still caught the salient points. "Can't say what I'd do in a similar situation, can I? I'm fairly certain I'd want to kill the piss-ant, though, and seeing as the boy was raised by Jack Stone, who clearly made an effort to train all three of his kids, I can't swear that I wouldn't have gone through with it, if I'd had the skills. For that matter, what if it had been your Ellie? Would you have just sat there and bloody well let her be raped by some hormone-driven bastard with a sense of entitlement to whoever and whatever he wanted?"

No. Morgan couldn't say he would have done that at all. Ellie, Rico's mother, had been his best friend all his life, right up until the day she'd died. She'd been the sibling he'd never had and he'd loved her more than anything. They'd been inseparable until he'd gone off to the Naval Academy, and when she'd called him in tears because she'd just found out she was pregnant because someone had presumably date-raped her with the help of pharmaceuticals, he'd been furious. It had been years later that he'd discovered the truth about the pregnancy and who, exactly, had caused it, and he and the FGC had taken down that branch of NovoTech, but he'd been angry enough to kill someone.

"I wouldn't have chopped them into parts," Morgan finally admitted, silently conceding that murder would likely have happened had he been there. "I just hate it that he threatened you. It makes me feel all...I don't know. Sick? Like I'd feel if someone threatened Rico or River, or even Moon, if that makes any sense."

Simon's eyes rolled just enough that Morgan knew it was happening when Simon turned away and left the shower. "Makes perfect sense, love," Simon answered, just as Morgan caught the towel the Brit had thrown at him. "Princess and I, we're your family. River is too, now. Moony...well, she's sort of our sister-in-law in a truly bizarre sense, yeah? Wouldn't be all sanguine if people started threatening you lot at random, either, so I'm right certain I get where you're coming from. Now use that towel and haul your lovely ass to our bed. Intend to plunder it a time or two before we're too worn out for fun and games."

That was actually the best offer Morgan had had since he, Simon and River had climbed from the bed that morning, and as Morgan wasn't a stupid man, he dried off and hauled his ass to bed with Simon an unseen but definitely felt heat behind him.

* * * *

Keeta — or Jericho, as she was more rightly called — was up on the Ranch with Patrice, looking at the new foal. After that, she would be staying with Patrice for the night, playing some weird fashion game, or so River had been given to understand.

He was still worried about Sky being nearby. He couldn't help it. After the mess River had needed to help clean up years earlier, he couldn't really think having Sky so close was a good thing. Except it had been so damned good to see his brother again. Such a relief to know Sky was still alive, because no matter what Sky had said about River never thinking Sky was dead, River actually *had* thought it. So much so that he'd mourned, in his own way.

That Sky wasn't dead had a part of River jumping with joy, but the rest of him was just waiting for more horror. It wasn't often that a guy had to help his brother hide the body of someone who'd once been a friend, after all, and while River had done exactly that — helped Sky hide the body components — he still remembered Carl Brown. The guy had only been a couple of years older than River, Moon and Sky when Sky killed him.

Carl had been a friend for a year or so, and River had thought the guy was decent enough until that third date with Moon. Back then, River would have beaten the crap out of Carl and sent him on his way, but Sky...

It had been the lack of emotion in Sky's face and voice when he'd asked River to help with the disposal that had convinced River his brother was a monster. In some ways he still felt that way. Carl had only been twenty. Maybe a beating would have taught the guy not to do that, but Sky had never given Carl that chance. He'd just killed him. Slowly, because the lower-body decapitation had happened first.

River still shuddered when he thought about dying that way, so yeah. Having Sky nearby created all sorts of mixed emotions for River. Knowing Keeta was up above and wouldn't be home that night, though? Oh, those emotions were anything but mixed.

The door to Morgan and Simon's rooms had been keyed to him already, and River was glad he'd just walked in, rather than knocking or anything, when he opened the door to Morgan and Simon's bedroom. What he saw right then wasn't something he'd ever want to interrupt, after all.

Morgan, on hands and knees in the middle of the big bed. Simon behind him, stabbing into Morgan with that amazing cock. Morgan grunting wildly every time Simon slammed deep. Simon's head thrown back, hips pumping wildly, small gasps River recognised leaving those pink lips with each thrust.

Simon wasn't close yet. River could tell by those tiny, hitched breaths. Simon got louder, the closer he came to spilling, and Simon wasn't loud yet. If River had to guess, he'd say they'd only been at it for a few minutes, at most.

His own cock was swelling rapidly, spurred on by each thrust River observed. Swelling and filling enough that his pants were more than uncomfortable and might even have qualified as a torture device.

"Oh, fuck." It was meant to be a whisper, but it came out as more of a loud-ass moan. That being so, River didn't bother trying to modulate his tone while he continued. "God, you guys are so fucking hot together!"

"Be even hotter," Simon said, slowing his thrusts enough that River could see the pace tormenting Morgan. "Be even hotter," Simon repeated, "if you got yourself naked and shoved that pretty cock of yours into our bloke's mouth, where it belongs. Or my ass, if you prefer, but Morgan's mouth needs less prep, yeah?" Then Simon smirked and tossed a wink his way, and River doubted that he'd ever stripped as quickly as he did right then. Not even the first time he'd gone to bed with his two lovers.

Morgan's mouth was just as ready and willing as River had known it would be. Just as wet and slick, too, and when Morgan moaned at the way Simon was fucking him, River felt it in his balls.

Simon was close enough that River could lean forward and kiss the man, and that was good, too. As always. Simon kissed almost as well as Morgan, and Morgan kissed like it was a divine calling, so 'almost' was still more than amazing.

Morgan's mouth was a dream, but that wasn't a surprise. The way Morgan worked his glans and frenulum, licked at his shaft and balls, still surprised River every once in a while, but not because he didn't know Morgan could do those things. The surprise was that Morgan wanted to. Even with knowing Morgan and Simon loved him, River hadn't quite managed to truly believe it.

He would. River was sure of that much. Maybe not that day or the next, but eventually he knew he would believe it. He would have to.

It was that last Game that had done it, River figured. The Game in Prague, where River had finally seen his brother again for the first time in years.

The Game that had driven Morgan to make love to him—because that was what it had been—without a condom for the first time. The Game that had led Simon to declare himself as River's man, too, and not just his handler.

Yes, they'd been sleeping together before then, the three of them, but the Prague Game had changed everything, and River was glad.

In a way, it had gone from being just another Game to being a Game of hearts, and as those hearts were his own, Morgan's, and Simon's, River couldn't really complain. Not even about Sky being nearby. Then Morgan's mouth moved harder on his cock and Simon's kiss went even deeper, and River lost himself in the sensations.

He pushed a cry between Simon's lips as he spilled rough and hard down Morgan's throat, and he swallowed Simon's shout just as Morgan's groan vibrated around his own softening cock.

A few minutes later, when he, Simon and Morgan had all collapsed and arranged themselves in a way that didn't involve noses in groins, River stroked one hand over Morgan's side, then Simon's because Simon was pressed up behind Morgan while River was facing them.

"So," River said simply, "I guess I'm going to put in a request for the rooms next door. As long as Keeta doesn't mind — and I guess she doesn't because she's the one who suggested it to you, Simon — I'm in. I love you guys. Not in the platonic way."

River knew his last words had been ridiculous even before Simon piped in with, "Fairly sure the rampant sex and continuing nudity gave that final bit away, love." Then Morgan jerked a little and Simon grunted. "Elbows in bed are bad manners, love!"

"So is making fun of one of your guys," Morgan said placidly, but the man was grinning. "What Simon meant to say was…yes. Move in next door. I'm not sure how easy it will be to make a connecting door because from what I understand this place was built to withstand a nuclear holocaust, but if it can be done, it will be done. Either way, you can come and go in our rooms as you please, and you're always welcome. Because we love you, River."

God, he was tearing up. He hadn't when they'd talked about it before, but right then River felt himself getting all misty-eyed. Then Simon made it worse.

"Morgan's right, love. Want you as close as we can get you. Door betwixt or not, you're part of us. Won't let that end, or take it for granted, yeah? Just love you, is all."

"All?" River sounded weepy even to himself. "That's *all*? That's fucking *everything*!"

It really, really was, and while River still didn't know what to do about Sky, or whether he, Morgan and Simon would manage to create a sustainable relationship between the three of them aside from their work, he believed they had a chance. He definitely loved them and he believed them when they said they shared the feeling.

Life in the FGC wasn't easy and there were no guarantees, but River had a feeling that he and his guys would manage to muddle through whatever life — or Games — threw at them. They were starting their very own Game. Their very own Game of Hearts.

Everything else mattered, sure, and River knew he would worry about Sky later, because Sky mattered too. But not as much as the love River had found so unexpectedly with the two men who made him feel complete.

He curled in closer, holding both his guys with the arm stretched over them, and when River drifted off it was with the knowledge that he would wake up with his future. That future was with the FGC but he had no problem with that. That future was also with his lovers, and that...? That made everything even more worthwhile.

River had never expected to find so much happiness, but he had, and one thing was for sure. He was never giving it up.

About the Author

Raised in and around Washington, DC, T.C. Blue doesn't write about politics. Years of working in various fields as a medical biller, motorcycle courier, hairdresser, retail slave, and chef (among other things) have contributed to T.C. being a "jack of all trades and master of none". She currently resides in suburban Maryland, far enough from the insanity of downtown Washington, D.C. for peace of mind, while close enough to dive into the craziness at will. It's a good life.

T.C. Blue loves to hear from readers.

You can find her contact information, website details and author profile page at http://www.total-e-bound.com.

Total-E-Bound Publishing

www.total-e-bound.com

Take a look at our exciting range of literagasmic™
erotic romance titles and discover pure quality
at Total-E-Bound.